MW01224395

21 stories

by
Peter J. Black

Dear Pavel,

Thak you for your interest in this book.
I hope you have as much fun reading it
as I did writing.

Peter J Black

This is a work of fiction. Names, characters, places, and incidents either are the product of the author's imagination or are used fictitiously. Any resemblance to actual persons, living or dead, events, or locales is entirely coincidental.

Visit the author's website at www.sapienoverlords.com

Introduction

21 stories from the Zzone is a collection of short stories situated within the Sapien Overlords universe. Some of them reveal the background of what happened before the Greatest War, a cataclysmic event that shook humanity to its core and brought a significant change to the world. Others deal with the consequences of that event, and the rise of the newly-established world government called the United Zzone Federation and its AI counterpart, Zetwork. A few remaining stories examine this project's future as humanity reaches for the stars and into the unknown galaxy. It would be difficult to imagine such a vast and unpredictable universe as is our own. As human beings, we tend to give anything unknown to us some human characteristics. Either we demonize or idealize those we come in contact with while projecting our thoughts and ideas onto them. Then, what if the world of tomorrow underwent a dramatic change that made it more accepting of different views and ideas and, at the same time, more despotic and authoritarian. What if the world had more human species than one? Could artificial intelligences ever be considered human or possess human qualities? These are the questions no one has an answer to, and this series tries to tackle them in unusual ways.

This collection is confusing as there is no better way to describe it. Suppose you are a reader who likes convoluted plots, inexplicable events and details that seemingly lead nowhere and, most of all, enjoy exploring the fragile nature of what is real. In that case, I suggest reading a few of these stories. Most stories are not highly speculative in a scientific sense, as the events described in them are probable and possible. On the other hand, what makes them unlikely is the social order we live in. Yet, as history demonstrated time and again, it doesn't take much for the pendulum to swing to the other side. And the pendulum of the Sapien Overlords universe has many sides. These stories can be considered to represent "the Absurd" in a sense, as the everlasting conflict between seeking an inherent value and meaning in life and the human inability to find any in this chaotic and irrational universe come together to ask a single question, what does it mean to be human? The answer to the question eluded even the greatest minds and is far too complex to be answered in short writings of fiction. Still, it is possible to think of certain aspects of being human, starting with biology, artificial intelligence, and our relation to nature and living organisms. Ultimately, the way we treat the world around us tells a lot about what we think of ourselves.

There is no particular order in which to read these stories as they are independent works of art and the representation below only states the chronological order in which they happen. There are references to certain events and notions that can help a reader better understand the world of Sapien Overlords scattered within these stories. This series is ordered by the publication date, not by the timeframe in which the stories happen presented below. The reason for this is entropy which guides our everyday lives.

1. Olympus Hill
2. Auto-brewery
3. Yawnrus
4. Planters
5. Continentopolis Australis
6. The trees remember
7. On the railroad
8. Lizard
9. One-armed Jack
10. Sapiens have returned
11. The castrates
12. Balkanizzonation
13. Interview with the vampires
14. Panem et circenses
15. 6 feet under
16. Under the pecan tree
17. New York, New York, Old Vegas
18. The man in the sphere
19. HMS
20. Glurbs
21. Nova

On the railroad

We are all born on the railroad. As children, we are taught that it is the only thing that matters and never deviates from its path. Because outside of the railroad, certain death awaits. Plumes of smoke are often seen in the distance, remnants of the Old World burning. Flying metal birds appear suddenly in the sky with screeching noise and disappear as fast. On some days, the wind brings an unfamiliar scent we talk about for days. On others, it brings fierce dust storms racing across the barren land. Cold nights and scorching days are a regular occurrence, no matter how far we progress.

On the railroad, we cross rivers, mountains, and old forests. We measure our lives in steps, progressing a certain number of them each day. In that way, step by step, we move forward. Sometimes it is the only thing that keeps us going, knowing that there is visible progress despite the railroad's food shortages and dangerous conditions. Little children, too, are aware that it is impossible to live outside of it.

When I was younger, I asked my father about the meaning of life.

"Follow the railroad," my father replied, "that is the only meaning you need. These tracks guide us. They provide us with shelter and nutrition. Eventually, we lay our bones on it to make the railroad stronger and the trip easier for the ones that come after us. We are the ballast that keeps the world turning."

"What is at its end? When will we reach our goal?" followed. Not receiving an answer for a while, I gave up asking. "I am tired of this constant walking in one direction. All I want is to run even for a second off the beaten track. Can I? Can I?"

The stern look on my father's face was answer enough.

My childish curiosity led me to ask all those meaningless questions. Of course, it wasn't possible to do so. Like all children, I was tired of listening about the scorched earth that bore no fruit, poisoned water that killed people who drank it in the most gruesome ways, and of stale air that suffocated within seconds. I desired freedom from all of that, from the same monotonous activities and the railroad itself.

Moments later, the look in his eyes changed, and he smiled. "Nobody knows. Those who have reached it never came back. So, it must be that is where paradise lies. But you have to believe in it, my son. You have to believe." My father continued his explanation by describing the place he knew nothing about as the one of pure bliss. A place where rocks bore fruit, where the water was so pure and teeming with life, the air you simply couldn't get enough of. His stories made me obsess with reaching that place, so much so that in an instant, I forgot about my desire to step off the railroad into the unknown.

I constantly pushed my already tired parents and the whole group to go faster, dragging them by the sleeves. Other children followed my example, eager to reach the promised land.

One time, several hours into the exciting campaign I started, a mishap occurred. It would have happened sooner or later, as the group never once traversed the land at such a pace. Ryan, one of the boys from the group, slipped on the sleeper and injured his knee.

"I told you we shouldn't be going this fast," his father told mine, before checking whether Ryan was alright.

His family immediately accused me of having something to do with that. They started asking questions they did not expect an answer to; they pushed my father and mother and made a scene as the whole group gathered around to listen. Some cursing was involved, but that is where it stopped.

"I am the one who decides how fast my family is going to walk. You take care of your own," my father replied calmly, but deep down, I knew his pride was hurt.

When the night fell, he entered the family tent and started beating me with his belt. Confused, I couldn't do anything but cry. He remained silent throughout the ordeal. Once he thought I had enough of it, he stopped. I was speechless. "You made a mistake, and now you need to suffer the consequences." Noticing I was still trembling, my bare behind as red as the corroded rails next to me, he almost apologetically added, "The world is unfair. The sooner you learn to deal with it, the better it will be for you."

The next morning I was woken up by the father. Still scared of him, I moved back to the corner of the tent. He brought breakfast and acted more politely than usual. There was no mention of the events that transpired the night before as if they had never happened. I did not dare talk about it as well, but I had a memory to remind me. The day was warm and windy as the endless journey continued. When everyone was expecting me to say something in my unusual fashion, I pretended to be distracted by the falling leaves. For the next few days, I mostly kept silent. My mind was burning with a question of why my father did what he did.

Windy days continued, and it was clear to most that Autumn was coming. On one particularly chilly day, I noticed some construction on the side of the railroad. It looked like a camp made by people traveling the railroad before us.

"It's ancient," one of the group's forward guards said. They were the bravest of us, those who swept the area before the rest of the group arrived.

"Undeniably deserted," the other one confirmed. The guards had a habit of speaking in short phrases to send the message faster.

"I will check to make sure. You wait."

We waited for a few minutes until he came back and told us it was safe to proceed. The previous occupants left behind some tools; one of the guards uncovered a working portable gas stove. With resources at hand, the group unanimously decided to spend the night in the camp and use the baking food stove to prepare food. After a long time, we were able to enjoy the taste of a warm, cooked meal.

The following day, one of the children did what was forbidden and stepped off the railway. It was Ryan, but it could have easily been me. I felt excited and somewhat happy it was him, thinking it was the right punishment.

Two of the scouts were selected, and following the footsteps, they stepped off the tracks and into the wilderness. It didn't take long to find him. Ryan was standing with his back turned to them, limping.

"What do you think you are doing there? Come back this instant, or I swear I will take you with me by force!" the irritated guard raised his voice, proving he too was human.

"But I, I needed to pee." His wet pants proved he wasn't lying, and his trembling voice showed how scared he was of the guards.

We all were; we had to be if we were to survive.

"Then I noticed a shining object in the distance and decided to follow it. But, but," Ryan shuttered, unable to finish the sentence. "I fell and hurt myself." The horror he saw that day scarred him for life.

The guards were perplexed by what the boy saw. "Now we know," the other one stated. "They all ended up on the pile here. Some poor bastard had to stay behind and finish the job."

What Ryan uncovered was the gruesome fact that most of the camp's previous occupants did not survive. There was a letter explaining the group's history and their tumultuous voyage across the wasteland. It said they decided to commit suicide rather than continue on this never-ending journey. When the guards came back, they ordered us to pack bags and leave the place immediately, leaving the half-eaten food and the burning stove behind.

Days later, I found out the truth, and all my resentment toward Ryan stopped. I only felt pity for him from then on. But I couldn't get myself to like him, no matter how much I tried. Our parents did their best to make us be friends again, knowing full well that the railroad was as deadly as the world outside it without company.

More death followed just a few kilometers ahead, and a scantily dressed body hung from a tree branch. Two more were ditched aside. It was not unusual to see such a sight, but it always brought along an ominous feeling. We came across bodies in many places, but never on the railroad itself. Before I had the chance to ask what had happened, the forward guard spoke, as if reading my mind.

"Mercy kills," he said. I understood the short and straightforward message as rather than dying of starvation and dehydration, disease, or cold; one of them decided to end the life of the other two.

"What catastrophe, what despair could make someone do such a thing?" I asked myself each time I saw the decomposing bodies. "What if the railroad is to blame? Was there a world where railroads did not exist? If not, what is at its end? Death? Another life?"

My father once told me there might be one; if you looked closely at the stars, you could find it.

I never understood what he wanted to say as whenever I looked up, I saw people looking down on us. We took the time to bury the unfortunate, the least we could do. It was a matter of honor, something we expected those who come after to do for us as well. The guards took their belongings, distributed them, and we left. There was no point in leaving the useful things to decay and rot. Nothing was wasted on the railroad; that was the only truth I ever knew.

Not as many days passed before we received another surprise. It was a living breathing person basking in the sunlight, followed by three dogs. He was not looking at the railroad, just walking around aimlessly.

"Best stay away from him," one of the guards said. "These Ascetics are dangerous."

"If he tries anything, we will handle it," another guard added, coming closer to him as the group slowed down to a near stop. These people were not a new sight, and the guards knew how to deal with them efficiently.

"What is Ascetic?" Thinking it was nationality or social status, I asked my father this silly question. Instead of an answer, I received a disapproving glance. My father waved me off and continued watching the strange man.

Several minutes later, the man came closer and caused a commotion among the group members. I was able to see him more clearly now; he had a long white beard and beads in his hair. His clothes were dirty, dogs malnourished, but content. I imagined he was such as well. He didn't say or ask anything of us, though many thought he'd look around for food or water. The guard took out some scraps from his backpack and left them beside the railroad. "Let's proceed," he said. And we did, without looking back, like sheep in a herd.

But I had to look back to see what kind of a man an Ascetic was. For a few moments, I was able to take a quick look before being hit on the head by my father. I found out nothing. He didn't approach the food at all, leaving it to his dogs to eat it ravenously. They were famished. I was wrong in assuming he was too because his face lit up when he saw the dogs feed. Several minutes later, we were already far away from that strange man. The howling of dogs was heard in the distance.

"A good sign," people argued.

"Three, that is a prime number," I heard someone in the group whisper so as not to alarm the guards. This kind of chatter was common whenever something unusual happened. For many, it was a way to share the pain or joy. "But taking them altogether, it counts as four which is not. Maybe that is why he is moving separately from them."

Someone else rejoined, "No, no, no. The dogs are, without a doubt, his pets. You always find meaning where there is none. Let's go now, the railroad ahead us is straight."

I wondered what pets were as I have never heard of such a thing. All animals are edible, some more than others, that is what my father taught me. Furthermore, he did not believe in numbers and their value other than for counting. He would say that quantifying your life experiences is not the right way to lead a meaningful life. Yet he too counted every step he took on the railroad. Nevertheless, I wondered how many times I did something in my life and whether I should keep track or just let go of that foolish idea.

At certain times, when the stars appeared to form a pattern or when the sky was clear, and there was no wind, our group took longer breaks from walking to perform a ritual. Sometimes it lasted a few hours, others several days. All adults had to participate in this communal experience, and children were put to sleep after a certain time passed. It involved, as it has for as much as I could remember, a combination of eating and drinking along with adults indulging in smoking some herbs that were considered a holiday treat. I found that smell obnoxious, revolting even. Very few talked about what it was, but its awful smell repelled us, children. The only thing I knew was that the morning after, I would wake up unusually relaxed.

"It's the spice," Ryan, still injured but on the road to recovery, said. "They use the spice. I heard it brings only happy memories and makes you forget about the bad things around us. I could use some of it now."

The other children, including me, agreed, as we had no idea what it was or how to use it. But we knew that if we tried to, we would be harshly beaten.

"It's not fair," another boy said. "We also deserve to be happy."

The following week, one of my friends jumped off the bridge, attracted by the water. Luckily, he was saved. We entered an area where suicides were common due to the high number of rivers crisscrossing the valley. That is what the guards presumed. Standing on the edge of a bridge, I looked at the river below. It was swollen from the rain that fell somewhere far away and vividly untamed, sparkling, and green. "Isn't life itself a constant balancing, paying attention not to fall off the railings?" I asked myself, paying attention not to take a wrong step and end up an integral part of the torrent. "Even if you make all the right moves, you can still be swept away in an instant." I peered down to take another, closer look. The abyss did not look back, and when my mother grabbed me by the sleeve, I moved away from this unrelenting force of Nature and back to the relative safety of the railroad. Another beating I earned in a short period.

These rivers also brought some joy as they were filled with edible fish. On that day, the final part of the ritual was conducted. What I remembered from the last one was a burning sensation that lasted for a couple of days. Adults were rushing around, unpacking the best or, in most cases, the only cutlery and dishes they had, setting up tables, one for food and the other for drinks, and getting dressed. But the most attention was paid to a singular item, a tree found nearby. I wasn't sure what they would do if there were no trees around. The ritual burning of the wood commenced as soon as the first stars appeared on the night sky. And the already familiar feeling of listening to some strange words the adults spoke came over me. My gaze was focused solely on the sparks flying up to the sky. The atmosphere was liberating. The elders were chasing away, invisible evil spirits as the guards monitored the railroad. It ended sooner than I'd hoped it would. And once again, I burned myself for coming too close to the fire.

We left the valley of the bridges and arrived at a plateau with many unusual jutting rocks extruding from the ground. Summits towering high above our heads were difficult to avoid and more laborious to pass. It felt as though every moment they would come crashing down on us. But the railroad as always provided safety and guided our way. We just needed to follow along its path, as we did our whole lives. I asked my father if I could explore around just a little.

"The railroad guides you, never steer away from its path," my father repeated daily.

For a moment, I believed he didn't say those words to me to keep me safe but to steel his resolution.

"Beware of the wind in this area," the guards warned. "If it blows this way, we are all doomed."

I wasn't exactly sure how wind could hurt any of us as the strong winds we faced before only managed to blow away some cloth and empty water bottles. I was frightened to the bone when I realized they were speaking in long sentences. They never did that, not even when death was imminent. Usually, one of them would just yell "Danger!" or "Stop!" and deal with whatever risk we were facing.

Except for this unknown looming threat, the whole area was uninteresting. The guards used some devices whose occasional crackling irritated my hearing. I learned from them; they were called Geiger counters and were used to pick up strayed radiation. This new knowledge invigorated my imagination as I have never heard of such a thing before. I tried imagining radiation as something shiny, a form of light. When I looked down at my feet, I saw the rails were gleaming in an unearthly manner and thought it was radiation. "What is this?" I asked my father.

"The plains are the most peculiar place," my father replied. "There are many rocks and stones. Some of them reflect different colors." He, too, gained the habit of speaking in short sentences.

Taking a closer look, I was able to see splinters and fissures on the ballast. It wasn't unusual to notice cracks in the wood, as the ballast supporting the rail track's weight was the most exposed part of the railroad. However, I didn't see these many cracks on such a small railroad area, ever.

My father noticed I was staring intently at the ballast. "Hot and dry weather does that to wood," he concluded.

I wondered what the weather would do to us if we stayed in that place long enough and wished we would leave as soon as possible. The rotting sensation never felt so strong. "I want to go!" I cried.

The guards heard me and approached. They, too, saw the cracks in the ballast. "We need to fix the fasteners before we can continue. Otherwise, they won't come," they ordered soon after that.

I knew well enough who it was they were talking about. Occasionally, a railcar came from afar, honked while passing us by, and left before we got the chance to take a proper look at it. Very rarely, it slowed down. But it would never take any of us with it. It was against the rules.

It was nearly impossible to fix the damage with the tools we had. People were frightened of the dunes, the sand, and the wind but continued working tirelessly to repair the railroad with everything they had. Just as predicted, the supply wagon came. It slowed down, and all of us managed to latch onto it, like breastfeeding babies. And not much unlike suckling animals, we all expected to get something from it.

There was no one and nothing inside except the desks and chairs. It was a fully automated model, and everyone felt disappointed. A calm and friendly womanly voice greeted us. I approached one chair and sat, looking out the window. A smiling face of a young woman materialized in front of me. Shocked, I almost fell off the chair. Moments later, I looked around. Everyone else was too busy looking around for useful things to notice her. Therefore, I decided to ask a very personal question. "What is the meaning of life?"

"Analyzing," the sound was heard. "Life is a comfortable and beautiful thing. By complicating it with unnecessary wants and desires, questions that cannot be answered, one only creates misery. It is better not to question the purpose of your existence."

That was the only thing the robotic woman said before once again disappearing into thin air. I waited for more, and when no more words came, I gave up hoping and stared out the window into the world outside the railroad. A machine couldn't provide me with the answer I sought to find. And if people and machines were clueless, who was I to ask?

Soon enough, the face of that same woman appeared on other desks as well. Everyone inside asked her questions and received similar answers. Excited, I reached the nearest one and repeated the question, but no answer came. All of the faces disappeared, and the woman's voice was no longer heard.

With no food or water inside, there was nothing keeping people interested, so we went out. My group was used to work, suffering, and taking no shortcuts. We strode off, looking at the speeding railcar disappearing in the distance. There were many more crossroads to come across and diverge, broken rail tracks to fix, rivers to disappear in, and bridges to cross. Or not. It took me a long time to figure out how to walk the line properly, and no matter how many times I wondered why I had to take this road, it never ceased to amaze me. The railroad.

One-armed Jack

"Daddy, why did you bring me here?" my son asked me as we were nearing the edge of the forest that once spread throughout the region and was now reduced to patches of trees that contrasted the bleak and barren land around.

"I want to tell you a story. You are now at an age when you can begin to understand it. Follow me," I said, pointing to the narrow path into the forest. We were in my hometown, which now belonged to a different Zzone, and just came back from visiting one of my childhood friends.

"But I am scared," he replied.

"There is nothing to be afraid of, not while I am with you. I know this forest like the back of my hand."

I followed the path inside, and he came after me. He wasn't feeling as comfortable as I was, being a child from the city after all. But I did my best to make him feel relaxed. We walked for a few minutes until I told him to stop.

"Just behind this tree is a place my friends and I would gather and play games, make plans, and imagine we were adventurers." There were four tree stumps still peering from the ground, a broken swing hanging from a branch, and a pit we used to make a fire in and bake whatever our parents gave us. "Take a seat," I told him as if greeting a guest. I, too, was a guest now.

"Okay," he followed the order without hesitation, still uncomfortable. After he looked around for clues, he asked: "Is this where you played with your friends when you were little?"

"Yes, I did. And we had a lot of fun. What is fun for children is not necessarily the same for adults." I stopped for a second, thinking about what to say next. After clearing my throat, I continued. "You see, there was this man called One-armed Jack."

"What was wrong with him?" my son asked. "Let me guess; he was bullying you? Well, luckily, I know how to handle a bully." He looked very proud when saying that. It was his way of showing himself and me he wasn't scared.

"I need you to hear this. And it's going to be a long story, so try not to interrupt." I felt inclined to say those words. "No one knew exactly how he lost his hand. Some believed it was in a freaky accident as a child; others thought it was a birth defect. Most adults didn't genuinely care and ignored his entire existence until bedtime when they used to scare children by telling stories of this strange man."

I noticed that for a moment, he twitched and paused. "Some said he tried to dig under a massive boulder in the forest to uncover a hidden treasure from before the Greatest War. A curse set by those who died on and around the boulder caused it to move. Losing an arm was his punishment."

"What was the cause?" he interrupted.

I ignored his question and continued. "Nature always takes back what belongs to it, the parents said to their children, so beware of what you do in the forest. This story served as a means of protecting them from animals or dangers they might get into, and no one, for a fact, believed One-armed Jack truly lost his hand that way. On the other side, no one asked him. If they did, he might have also told them the truth."

"How did he lose it?" He was persistent.

"I am not sure I ever knew the true reason. His real name was not Jack, but everyone called him that anyway. He wore ragged clothes and one of a kind straw hat, but he was no shepherd. The children yelled hillbilly when they saw him. They would often make scornful remarks on rare occasions he encountered them. On occasions, he had to chase them off his property. He had quite a few acres to spare, and at the time, this was a lush forest. Children can be very mean when inclined to." I looked directly into his eyes to make sure he was following what I was saying.

"How many of you were there?" my son asked as a reply to my sudden reaction. He realized I was talking about myself.

"Five in total," I said, showing five raised fingers, the same way I did as a child when asked to count something. "Lefty, Ethan, Jacob, Noah, and I. Some girls would join us from time to time when we had bigger plans. Mainly we kept to ourselves. Lefty's real name was hard for us to pronounce as his family moved in from a faraway Zzone before he was born. They kept some traditions of the Old World, including naming children. But I think it started with the letter P. We called him Lefty because he was left-handed."

"There were other children besides us naturally, children from the other side of the forest. They were particularly angry with One-armed Jack as his property extended far into their own. Their parents wanted the land for themselves. When they failed to achieve their goal and provoke the reaction they hoped they would, it was easy to let their children off the leash. Can you do anything with just one hand? The loudest among them would declare. How do you hold your pants while you pee? No wonder you are all alone would follow. Yet one-armed Jack did not reply even when the children hurled pebbles and small rocks at him."

"Why didn't he retaliate? He had every right to do so. He should have done the same!" my son raised his voice, taking the side of the One-armed Jack.

"He was just like that, especially towards children as he didn't have his own. You will understand when you get older. At one time, a pebble hit his window and broke it. The children backed off and ran into the forest. They ran back to their parents, who gave them a beating for coming so close to One-armed Jack. We were watching him on the other side. One-armed Jack flinched for a second as if remembering a familiar cracking sound and resumed his daily work. He did not chase after them as he knew their parents' punishment would be enough. The broken window remained such until much later when the cold days came, and he had to fix it."

"Jack was pretty lonely, wasn't he? I mean, he must have been, if he allowed those children to do as they wished."

"Though he did not keep animals, a limping disheveled dog could often be seen in his yard. The dog was named Arab. I once heard he named the dog after his friend from the military, but I now realize that it was just another made-up story. And that dog had his own stories to tell. He, too, was chased, attacked, and poisoned once but managed to live through it all. "If only dogs could speak, "I told myself, "they would have much greater things to say than men." He was his only friend."

"Well, those children certainly were not his friends." My son was still angry at the children for treating One-armed Jack that way.

I had to tell the story at the risk of disappointing my son. "None of the children were, but we did not hate him. You know, I wasn't that good myself." I tried to sell this with a smile, but my son did not seem to be buying it. Still, I had to tell the truth. "It was around springtime we had a break from school, and we decided to do one of our traditional seasonal raids on One-armed Jack's apiary. The only reminder of the cold days behind were the trees whose leaves began to change color. And our target was the early season cherry trees. Fresh and passionately red cherries acted as a lure for the boys and girls still learning about life's secrets. As any combat force, our first task was to neutralize defenses, and we did that by throwing a cooked bone Lefty stole from home to Arab. He took the bait, and Lefty stayed behind watching over him. When the infiltration was completed, we proceeded to feast on the sweet-savory and warm cherries. Like trained professionals, we assigned roles. Ethan and Jacob were to keep a close watch and warn the others in case One-armed Jack appeared. Noah and I were the fittest in the group, so we climbed as fast as we could. Knowing full well time was of the essence, we grabbed as many as we could. After having a mouthful of happiness, we wanted more and started eating cherries that were not ripe enough. We ate until our bellies hurt and then more. No branch was spared, no cherry left untouched."

"Dad?" my son was puzzled. "That's not you, that can't be you. I don't know you like that. You never once stole anything in your life."

He was disappointed; I knew that. "But I was, and I did." Then, trying to move the topic away from me, I continued. "Little did we know that One-armed Jack carefully kept a close watch on us. His main concern was that his trees were not damaged. Mere minutes after the initial strike, the only remaining cherries were the ones at the top. They were also the largest and tastiest of all, as it usually is with things in life. Two boys, whose rivalry began a long time ago, decided by just looking at one another to start a contest. Who would climb the tallest branch first and win? To the victor go the spoils or, in that particular case, the cherries. Noah and I climbed as skillfully as we could, disregarding the crackling branches beneath our feet. Then one of the branches snapped. To this day, no one knows which one and who fell first. The other children, fearing

One-armed Jack's retaliation more than the fall or injury, didn't look at the cherry tree. They ran as far as legs could take them, leaving the two of us behind." I took a look at my son; he was about to say something but stopped. "You can tell me; I won't get angry. It is my past."

"You were a real jerk!" my son accused. He was disappointed.

"I was, I was indeed." I scratched my head and looked down at the uncut grass, downhearted. "Our eyes were focused on his house. I think I understand his reaction back then, and him better now. He couldn't let one of the children get hurt in the stampede that would result from him coming out of the house, but he also couldn't stand aside and just watch his precious plants destroyed. We heard a gruntle and saw One-armed Jack staring at us from the windowsill. He adjusted the straw hat and started making noises as if breaking things inside, which only added to his wild man's appearance. We had enough time to escape before he came out. Arab almost immediately appeared as if ordered to do so and started chasing after us. He would have been a great shepherd's dog in another life. The dog's courage made up for his old age, and we narrowly escaped by climbing over the fence. Lefty was already out with his clothes ripped. Ours were soaked red with fruit juice. Arab took some time to jump over the fence then continued chasing after us. Hearing the sound of his master, he stopped and returned as if nothing had happened."

My son was speechless, and I knew his silence spoke more than words ever could.

"Much to our surprise, one day we found out he was gone. His place was empty, with only Arab keeping watch. At first, we thought he died in the house as he had no family that we knew of. But as the days went by and no smell came from the surrounding area, we assumed he went somewhere and decided to break in. Almost immediately, everyone prepared for the coming operation. It was of the essence to do it fast before the other group found out. But the plans had to be sped up as Lefty overheard a rumor that One-armed Jack was bound to return within days. Therefore, a small group of boys was to sneak into the enemy territory at night. Taking precautions, we brought chicken legs with us in addition to the bone usually given to Arab.

"No one's ever been inside his house," Ethan said.

"That is why I will be the first one," Jacob added.

"Yeah, right after me," Noah confirmed.

"Not if I am already there," I concluded.

"Lefty was silent. He didn't like the plan very much. As always, his role was to stay behind and take care of Arab.

Everything was going according to plan, and we were about to enter the shed attached to the house. The door was not locked, and we opened it carefully, not wanting to make any noise just in case. There were gardening tools and machines inside it. Some items were covered in dust; others had noticeable signs of recent usage. We slowly crept through the darkness until Ethan lit a match. He was always the first one to react."

"There is nothing here but garbage," Noah surprisingly exclaimed.

"The others wanted to silence him, but realizing it is probably too late for that, they changed our minds. Instinctively all of us turned back, expecting One-armed Jack to appear out of nowhere and attack. But he wasn't there, nor Arab. Lefty was doing a good job keeping him fed and satisfied.

"Wait, there is something in the back," Jacob said.

"Behind the tools and the machines lay an indefinable mound of things covered in cloth. We knew what to do at that moment without saying it. I unwrapped the fabric carefully as if opening a birthday gift. I found a shining but rusty military helmet and a jacket of the same olive-green color to my utter astonishment. Below it was a toolbox. The wind outside turned violent, threatening.

Wooden boards of the old shed made a horrific sound while the doors unhinged and fell.

"He is here," my three friends and I all screamed in panic.

"I was scared stiff. At that moment, I felt as though I would die. This intangible feeling, the instinct to run away from the unknown, was blocked by an even greater fear of the danger One-armed Jack was. A few moments later, I joined the group, now a mindless mob, rushing towards the fence, hitting and stomping on one another. Lefty, who was still guarding Arab, saw us and began to scream. We all ran as fast as we could while Arab, dazed and surprised by the sudden noise, rushed back into the shed. We were stuck between a rock and a hard place, but no one flinched, not even Lefty, who, after the initial scare, looked stern and serious. As soldiers, we were embarrassed about showing fear and blushing in dishonor."

"Run," Ethan said, panicky. That was enough to make the rest of us follow, as if accepting an order we eagerly awaited.

"I will be back, I screamed in anguish and fear, eager and determined to see what was hidden inside the toolbox. Such a public promise made in despair only served to strengthen my determination to find out what mysterious items Jack kept hidden away."

"In the following days, we were thinking of a plan that would enable us to steal the whole toolbox and like pirates take it away and hide it somewhere. We would sell the things we did not need and keep or share those we desired. Every one of us imagined the toolbox contained what he desired. Most wanted hidden treasures, Lefty said he hoped there were books inside, and I was thinking of toy weapons.

"What happened then?" my son interrupted after a long pause. "Did you find anything?" He no longer seemed upset at all. Moreover, he was eager. That reminded me of me in his age.

I was too involved in my reminiscence to see his rising interest in the story. "The final plan was set in motion, and we solemnly swore that after we attained the toolbox, we would no longer have anything to do with One-armed Jack. Like all good plans, it was straightforward and simple. It was the same as the previous one, with one difference. This new attack would happen during the day to avoid unpredictable situations."

"One-armed Jack is gone, and who knows when and if he will ever return," Noah, my rival, reasoned. "And if he does, we will be able to see him in time."

"We felt a slight breeze coming from the north as we approached One-armed Jack's house. Rustling leaves and crackling of the branches seemed to warn us of something. The toolbox was standing in the open, the cloth we previously removed missing. The sun was breaking through the gaps in the boards that covered the shed. Everything seemed ideally placed to reinforce that glorious moment of triumph. The toolbox's rough and scratched surface represented the dilapidated state of disrepair of One-armed Jack's shed, house, and the world. The locking hinges screeched as I opened the toolbox."

"Aand?" my son asked impatiently. "What did you find inside?"

"Much to my surprise, it was filled with documents, drawings, and what appeared to be letters. Others soon joined, their eyes gleaming with excitement. Though these documents contained no monetary value, they were a real hidden treasure."

"Stop! Don't do it! A voice seemingly coming from nowhere was heard yelling. It resonated through the air, finely tuned by the structure of the shed. Someone was in the house. With such an unexpected turn of events, we didn't have the time to react. We didn't account for someone else being present and instinctively turned our heads to what we determined was the source of the yelling when we saw him, the bad guy himself. Out of all the people in the world, One-armed Jack was staring through the window. I quickly grabbed the first thing I found inside the toolbox, hoping to at least snatch something to brag about later and ran."

"He is going to kill us this time for real," Ethan yelled.

"And no one is ever going to find us," Jacob added.

Noah had nothing to add and only repeated, "He is, he is."

"Run you fools," I said, overtaking them. "Don't just stand there." We ran as fast as our legs could take us.

"When we jumped over the fence, we saw one-armed Jack entering the shed to assess the damage. I quickly looked at the thing in my hand. It was an old photo of a group of soldiers. I could have never imagined One-armed Jack was young as we only knew him in his old age, but he was there in the photo with two hands. The next moment I saw him approaching with incredible speed."

"What happened next? Did he catch up to you?" the excitement in my son's eyes showed he cared for me. "I hope he gave you a proper beating," but mostly, he had sympathy for old Jack.

"The things that followed, many would later say, were inevitable. For the first time since we could remember, One-armed Jack left the confines of his estate to come after us. And he chased us ruthlessly through the thick forest, neglecting the overgrowth and occasional sharp rock he stepped on. He finally reached up to us in the one place we knew he avoided visiting, the boulder. It was the site of our base, and the campfire there was still smoldering and smoking. We were all frozen from fear and scared to death. One-armed Jack grabbed the closest one to him by the hand, Lefty, and shook him.

"Where is it?! Where is it?! Who has it? He yelled at all of us. How could you do this?! All of you, how, why would you do something like that? There were noticeable signs of confusion and disturbance on his face. The look in his eyes was scarier. For those couple of moments, I was sure I would die. And then One-armed Jack let go of Lefty's hand. When he did that, we all started running again, but the man had no intention of chasing after us."

"I was so scared I forgot I dropped the photo at the base, around the boulder. As I turned my head to look at him, I saw One-armed Jack on his knees. He was staring at something on the ground. And then he started hitting himself on the head wildly until there was blood. The last we saw of him was when he placed his blood-covered palm on the boulder. We were already far deep into the forest. Many days later, the rumor spread that Jack's army buddies rose from eternal slumber beneath the boulder, and as ghosts came back to haunt and perhaps take him with them. We never went back to his place again and abandoned our base. What was the truth no one could tell as all those moments are lost to history now."

"Dad?" my son asked. "How did One-armed Jack lose his arm?"

"Many years later, long after One-armed Jack died, and we grew up, we found out the truth. Jack was an army decorated veteran suffering from PTSD. We learned that his platoon, his herd was long gone, his friends butchered in the war and left behind on the battlefield. His arm was amputated when a bomb he tried to deflect exploded. He carved out their names in that boulder with his one remaining hand as a memory to them. The Greatest War had many mysteries of its own, and although the world around him crumbled and ended, One-armed Jack still had something to hold onto. That is why I brought you here today to remember this moment and never forget your roots even when the times are hard. Even when I am gone."

The castrates

Humanity strived to reach utopia for centuries, and when it finally did, didn't know what to do with it. Some sacrifices had to be made to maintain social order and keep the system running. In certain Zzones, the laws regressed and resembled those from the past, if not worse. One such example was the infamous Nebraskan Zzone, which, surrounded by more powerful and prosperous Zzones, struggled to survive in the ever-changing political climate.

Sexual relations were prohibited to improve productivity, and people were rewarded for reporting any impure thought, whether it was theirs or someone else's, to the authorities. Specialized personnel was trained and created by advanced technology to protect the privacy of those involved and avoid public scrutiny. These genetic enhancements allowed their memories to be stored and removed on request. They were called castrates and served various functions, most notably as law-enforcers.

It is important to note that at the time of its formation, the United Zzone Federation presented merely a loose conglomerate of Zzones that accepted any rule, as long as they were mostly following its goals. Nebraskan Zzone was one of the more unusual and unstable additions to it. It was a suitable place for the development of such unorthodox doctrines due to historical circumstances. It valued the sanctity of the human body above all and in no way supported acts of physical castration. Mental castration, on the other hand, was welcomed with open arms.

As far as anyone was concerned, John was an ordinary man. Living in what used to be called the Midwestern United States, he craved the things all men and women did in not so small Union City. More things, more power, and more ways to use that power. And like any other law-abiding citizen, he kept himself busy to avoid any sexual thoughts. Such actions were much approved and sponsored by the leadership of his company. "After all," he thought, "it is much better to do more work, to exercise more, to contribute in any way than to be chemically castrated again."

All citizens were required to pass the maturity test at the age of thirteen. Those who did not were given another chance after being chemically induced to control themselves. In most serious cases, young adults were forced to spend weeks or even months in correctional facilities until their hormonal levels were stable enough. Physical removal of the genitalia was a sin, and no lives were ever officially taken. It was considered a waste of society and productivity to do something like that.

On Wednesdays, John would take a twenty-mile run with his colleague, Molly, for whom he had a lot of respect. He regarded her as an exemplary specimen and often praised her physical aptitude. Molly could run more than John, but due to some sympathy, which they both considered completely asexual, she would pretend to get tired around the last mile and ask John for support. John, on the other hand, graciously provided it, following the rules of camaraderie. They were both unfamiliar with the concept of flirting, yet that is what they did every Wednesday. As much as they or anyone could tell, there was nothing remotely sexual in their weekly ritual. Still, they both felt a certain buzz the day before Wednesday.

Fearing that something or someone would bring an end to their routine often made them worried, so they tried to keep six feet apart distance at any given moment. Or maybe it was just the aftermath of the luring "vaccine" they had to receive as children. That is why every Tuesday, both of them performed certain rituals of self-purification, which involved either mental or corporeal form of self-punishment. This specific Tuesday, Molly felt strangely confident about herself and decided not to perform the sacred act.

When the two souls met, the air around them felt dense, and they both started sweating. That is when Molly realized something was different about John. His reserved attitude, she not only respected but admired professionally, seemed unusually relaxed. An outlandish, raw fragrance was coming from him. "He changed something. A new perfume? Or is this how he usually smells." She could not help but feel a particular heat inside her penetrate the walls of self-control she so meticulously built. "Control yourself, Molly, you are better than this." She looked away but suddenly felt weak at the knees.

"Are you okay?" John asked her, feeling her gaze shifting away. "We don't have to do it today if you are not up to it."

His kind words further strengthened the feeling that was rapidly growing inside her. There was a fire in her eyes burning as bright as the star above them, and he could feel it.

It was at that moment John found himself thinking something no law-abiding, honest man would. He thought about kissing her in front of all their colleagues so the whole world could see and began to sweat extensively. But he managed to restrain himself, clearing his thoughts with a loud grumbling noise, not much different from that of a primate. It was so intense some of their coworkers immediately turned their heads to observe what would happen next.

Molly gestured to John to begin their weekly stroll.

He scratched his head in confusion, then followed suit.

They continued walking down the boulevard in the same way as any other Wednesday but with a noticeable tension in the air. Their usually harmonized movements were out of balance, and they often stumbled along the way. For the first few miles of their run, they managed to keep the appearance of a fully functional team. Then, approaching a conveniently narrow path, they accidentally touched elbows. Any physical contact other than that approved by the government was not allowed and severely punished. Any citizen wanting to keep their status in the society would report this to the castrates office. However, there was no one around, but the two of them. So if they agreed this hadn't happened, no one would suspect them. Even though they touched inappropriately on accident, they both felt ashamed for allowing such a thing to happen.

"Should we report this?" John asked, emphasizing the word should.

"It is the right thing to do," Molly replied without giving a hint of whether she wanted to do it or not.

Her hesitation was a sign to John that they should not. "There is too much paperwork anyway," he replied, signaling he was against it. He was aware that reporting it would mean a reduction in salary and an unpaid day off he couldn't afford at that time.

Molly and John continued their weekly stroll, which was slowly turning into a full-fledged hike. Soon they began to run. It didn't matter whether it was because that is what they usually did or the fear of repercussions that being caught lying would bring. There was something more to it. Their brains began to release hormones that improved their speed, focus, and agility at the usual time like any other Wednesday. Yet this time, they suspected their bodies reacted to certain stimuli.

Before they knew it, John was kissing her as passionately as he could, realizing the true meaning of his life, his purpose. On the other hand, Molly surrendered herself to the feeling of her body's desire and let go of all the constraints society imposed on her. Like the birds on the trees around them, they too began to sing the song of love. There was no time for words anymore; they were meaningless. There was no time to check if anyone was watching them.

Unaware of what a kiss truly meant, Molly feared she would get pregnant from it. It was so quickly forgotten that people booed and yelled at pregnant women for being and doing what Nature intended them to do before their time. These often erupted into protests or punishments for those women as they were considered unclean and animal-like for failing to control their urges. No one minded the dark side of such actions as women were forced to give up their holiest, the sanctity of their bodies, and undergo dangerous procedures to cure themselves of this one remaining ailment of humankind. That was such a long time ago as now the penalty for suspected unapproved pregnancy, they knew, was death at sight. In exceptional cases, these women were allowed to pay their debt to society by giving birth to children of upstanding citizens. Repopulation was achieved through the use of artificial wombs, presented as "the cleanest and the only scientifically approved method."

Moments or minutes later, instead of progressing further, they suddenly stopped touching. A loud sound from somewhere in the distance interrupted their lovemaking. It would be anyone's guess if they knew what step to take next. A strange yet familiar sensation embedded deep within

John's mind made his skin crawl. He stepped away from Molly for just a tiny fraction of a second to clear his thoughts. At that moment, they gazed upon each other and realized their hidden desires, their true feelings. They knew they were meant for each other.

The sound became louder, reaching miles away. Both John and Molly covered their ears, keeping six feet apart, as was the rule. Iron-clad operatives with the crossed-out pregnant woman insignia on their shoulders appeared from the bushes and the trees around. John understood something inside of him decided he was the one to take all the blame, to make a stand and defend the woman he loved. He raised his hands in the air, not in surrender but protest, and looked at the group of men approaching them.

"Careful, this one is not going to go down easily," the commanding officer said.

"Roger that," the other men replied incongruously. They pointed their weapons at the eloped couple, preparing to shoot.

In the meantime, Molly grabbed John's waist and decided she was never going to let go of him. Her love for him, like an addiction, was the sweet forbidden fruit that, once tasted, could never be forgotten. "I will never leave you," she cried.

He looked at Molly and immediately regretted not having touched her or kissed her the first time he saw her. He wished he could have taken all those moments back. Then, using his left arm, he hugged her, to protect her from the attack. It somewhat appeased his aggressive stance. But the fire in his eyes was burning very strong.

The first bullet only grazed her cheek, while the second one hit John's arm. What followed was a series of shots aimed directly at him. Unable to hold back, John's eyes began to tear until he finally fell to the ground, still soft and muddy from their blood. "Run," he yelled, "run before they get you too!"

Molly was dumbfounded as her initial reaction was to run. Yet, the fight-or-flight response of her body shifted rapidly towards the other side. She was about to fight back instinctively; she wasn't going to give up her life for nothing. There were two men behind Molly that she was unaware of. The officer began to approach her as she stood her ground, clenching fists and grinding teeth. Like a wild animal, she was about to jump and tear him to shreds. The commanding officer stopped at a certain distance allowing the two men he sent to grab her by the hands and immobilize her. Molly screamed in anguish, spitting at the officer who was now very near to her. The other officers were beating and kicking

John, who was already losing the battle. Molly closed her eyes and tried to shut off her ears with no success.

"This is your punishment. Look at him. You can't lock it away like some unwanted memory; it will always be with you until the very day you die," the commanding officer spoke to Molly as two operatives forcibly held her.

From the tight grip she was in, the bones began to crack and break. She screamed in anguish.

All the while, John was lying on the ground, immovable.

Finally, taking a look at him, the commanding officer said: "With all their freedom, birds are bound to fall to the ground and die eventually." He lost interest in Molly, and came closer to John and squatted in front of his beaten-up body.

Unable to speak, John was only able to see glimpses of the man's neck and a tattoo that had two intertwined letters Z. He had already forgiven him. As the warm blood was slowly making its way out of his body, John remembered all the pleasant short moments with Molly. He did not regret his decision even when the operative's bullet made its way through his skull. At the end of his life, he could not comprehend what he felt for Molly, what he experienced, and ultimately dreamt of. John only knew of love.

Molly, on the contrary, could and would never forgive. Her agony became more intense by the minute. Raging madness ensued. Molly's inhumane, unearthly screams, rattled everyone around her, even the cold-blooded commanding officer. It was already too late, as John had passed away. "Kill me, too!" she shrieked, "Kill me, or I will kill all of you!"

"Honey, you ain't gonna die today," the officer calmly replied. There was no trace of emotion on his face. "A trial awaits you. And after that, who knows? It would be a waste to destroy such a valuable body."

He pointed to the man far back dressed in civilian clothing. It was one of her closest colleagues. Molly realized he saw everything and recorded it in his memory as evidence. After all, she concluded, anyone could be a castrate.

The man in the sphere

It was just an ordinary autumn day in Central Park, New York. The idyllic scenery of people walking their dogs, families with children and those without strolling up and down the narrow paths and people jogging was suddenly interrupted. Birds were tweeting and chirping, squirrels, ducks, and geese eating their daily meal, pigeons made a mess as they usually do. Everyone else was going about their daily routines.

The whole world stopped for a moment as a spherical, translucent object materialized over their heads.

"This was not here yesterday, was it?" one of the confused people present at the site asked.

"It must be some new avant-garde art installation. I wonder who gave them permission to install it here?" the other one replied.

These first innocent reactions were followed by louder, more violent cries of fear and awe. Mothers and fathers grabbed their children, couples ran hand in hand, and joggers sped up their pace. Only the animals paused for a moment but soon enough returned to their daily habits. They were not afraid of this new and unknown menacing object hovering above their heads. It is true that after all, only people fear what they don't understand.

Law enforcement soon arrived at the scene, but their arrival was delayed by the usual crowdedness widely known and recognized as one of the city's symbols. Unlike its Hollywood-style representations, their appearance was not as swift and chaotic. The police cars did not drive over grass and trees and instead orderly parked around the Park's emptied area. Another sudden appearance exacerbated the terrible traffic conditions in the Big Apple, turning it effectively into a jungle. All around, people were puffing and panting, some of them yelling. But most were just worried whether they would get to work on time. As they pointed their weapons at the unidentified hovering object, the police were dumbfounded by how inert and immovable it was. It is as if it were there all along. The sphere blended into the surrounding area, occasionally turning silvery and reflecting the officers' faces that were gazing at it.

"What do you think it is?" one of the officers asked his colleagues. His voice was rough but scared.

"Aliens. What else could it be?" the other one replied confidently.

"Out of all the places on the earth, they always attack New York," the third one added, feeling the need to join in the conversation. He was about to recap all disaster movies set in New York when another patrol car arrived at the scene.

"Are you the first responders to the scene?" the officer running towards them asked. "What is the situation?"

They turned around and realized that he was not an ordinary policeman by looking at his clothes and insignia. He was either a deputy or someone more significant. "Everything clear, sir, officer Murkowski" the men unanimously replied after reading his nametag. "No activity from the unidentified object whatsoever."

Not satisfied by their answer, Murkowski raised his voice and yelled at them. "Who the hell can tell me what is going on here?! I don't need these generic answers. Tell me what you do know for crying out loud."

"S-sir," one of the three officers observing the situation replied shakingly. "S-sir, this unidentified hovering craft of some sort appears to be inactive. We suspect it might be extraterrestrial in origin."

"No, shit! I can see as much with my own eyes." He took a deep breath to relax, striking them with his gaze. "Have you contacted the National Guard? Anyone? Did you do anything but sit here in wait like a group of idiots?"

"B-but," all three of them shuddered at the thought of Murkowski lashing out at them. "B-but sir, we only just got here."

"I don't care!" Murkowski yelled. "Set the perimeter this instant, you hear me!?" The men instantly rose and turned towards the unknown hovering object. One could almost feel their trepidation as the clattering and rattling of handcuffs followed their every move. They held up to them, carefully approaching the sphere that was still very far off.

"Excuse me, gentlemen," a mysterious man approached them from behind and said in a carefree manner, " but could you let me pass. I am afraid I am terribly late for my afternoon nap." Already alarmed, officers turned around and just stared at him, frozen.

"How can someone so casually approach us, seeing how there are sirens and all," the officers talked among themselves.

"Now who the hell are you?!" asked Murkowski, preparing to take out his weapon and point it at the man. "Leave the premises this instant! Do you hear me?"

The three officers just stood silent, waiting to see what was going to happen next.

"Why?" the man asked, seemingly confused. He did not exhibit any signs of the slightest distress or discomfort.

"Well, don't you see that strange-looking object ahead?" Murkowski composed himself a little after receiving that kind of reaction. "It materialized from thin air. We do not know what it is or what it wants from us."

"So?" the man calmly replied.

"It is not safe for you to stay here. Do you understand?! The army is expected to arrive here at any moment now."

Not heeding to the officer's warning, the man simply ignored him and proceeded towards the sphere.

"Stop, you hear me?! Stop, or I will shoot!"

But the man did not stop. He continued pacing the same way as before.

Murkowski did as he promised and shot a warning shot into the air. The three officers ducked and moved away. But the man continued walking.

2.

As expected, the appearance of an unknown hovering object resembling a silvery sphere was a big event for the city. At first, no one dared approach it, and the military strictly prohibited any close contact. Central Park was sealed off, and military installations brought to monitor the sphere. However, this action did not go lightly with the sphere's inhabitant, who found all of the racketing and noise annoying.

"In all honesty, New York is a busy and bustling city with its own set of deafening sounds, but at least I am used to those. But this, this is outrageous." The man repeated, looking down on Central Park from the sphere. After the police officers' initial contact, he entered the sphere from below, pulled up by something resembling a tractor beam.

Three officers reported the event to their superiors, who said such a thing was impossible and that the sphere had a psychological effect on them. It was expected that at least someone had recorded something happening to show it as proof. Officer Murkowski unsuccessfully called in the National Guard and only managed to reach local authorities for help.

Still, the city's hectic daily traffic situation made people only focused on their own lives and how to get as fast as possible from home to work and vice versa. It took some days for the special team to assemble most of the equipment and start communicating with this strange person. He was thought to be either an alien or a time traveler. Most citizens felt unsafe but carried on with their lives.

Murkowski took upon himself to be the primary negotiator. He began by asking several useless but straightforward questions.

"I am neither," the man replied when asked about his origin. He sent his answer in the form of a paper plane. He was not used to dealing with peering eyes and wanted to avoid publicity at the risk of becoming a celebrity. For some reason, he couldn't understand why all that attention was focused on his house and him in particular. "Leave me alone," he finished. But Murkowski was relentless and insisted on talking with him. "What do you want me to say!" the man shouted through the opening in the sphere, which resembled a window.

"We just want to talk," the reply came from Murkowski holding a megaphone. It echoed the Park, scaring off the birds and other animals.

The man did not reply.

Another day passed, and he agreed to come out of the sphere, but there was just one person present only on condition. He was starting to feel increasingly trapped inside, unable to complete his daily tasks and habits. The authorities agreed, leaving only one negotiator behind. Officer Murkowski was removed due to his "aggressive and unsatisfactory" negotiating technique. The National Guard was brought in.

When he was entirely sure there was no one else in the Park, animals and wildlife aside, the man descended the same way he entered the sphere, through its bottom. The first thing he noticed about the person waiting for him at the round table was a black suit. Compared to him, the man was dressed casually, wearing an autumn sweater and a beanie as it was getting colder. He approached the chair and sat without saying a word.

"Allow me to introduce myself, my name is David Botcher, and I am…" he was interrupted before finishing the sentence.

"I am not interested in getting to know you," the man interjected. "I don't plan on being your friend, and I don't think you want to be mine. So say what it is you want and leave me alone."

"Wow, you speak fluent English," Botcher said, less in surprise and more for trying to ease the situation. It was one of the negotiating tactics he was taught in school.

"Well, of course, I do, I am a New Yorker. But I suppose you wouldn't know anything about that," the man pointed out, catching a glimpse of Botcher's southern accent.

Botcher was surprised by that unexpected reaction. In his belief, only New Yorkers dared reply in such a prideful way. But he wasn't ready to believe him just yet. "For starters," he smiled cautiously, "I hope you don't mind me asking, but who are you? What is that silvery looking sphere behind us? Is it extraterrestrial in origin?"

"What do you mean, who am I? I already told you." The man was irritated by this assumption. "I live here, and this is my home. You are the aliens, in my opinion. People like you just coming uninvited and start asking questions, invading my privacy. Do you even know how difficult it is to get by without all of you imposing yourselves on me? You brought the National Guard. Who told you to do that?"

"I personally did no such thing," Botcher tried to clear his name once again. "But I understand your frustration with the whole situation. It is just that everyone is so curious to see what that sphere is."

"It is my house. I already told you that. You are welcome to visit it if you wish, but I must warn you I do not like crowds much in particular. I may if I decide you are just wasting my time."

That was the sign Botcher was waiting for. The man finally gave in under pressure. "Can I bring my camera and record the inside of your house? I believe many people would like to see the inside of the sphere, I mean your house," he corrected himself. It was never a bad idea to be overly cautious, not with this man who probably had superhuman powers.

"Most certainly not," the man replied. "What am I to you? A reality TV star? A famous actor or singer? Some kind of celebrity? No, I do not agree with that."

"Well, in a way, you are a celebrity," Botcher tried to clarify. "Your appearance, along with this mysterious sphere, caused people to think of conspiracy theories ranging from government experiments to aliens. Most of them are unimaginative, I can tell you that, but still, we too are unsure of who exactly you are."

"I'm alive flesh and blood man, same as you, same as millions of other people in this city. There isn't any mystery in that," the man replied calmly. "I will not agree to any tests if you try to force me."

"I can guarantee you we won't, at least for the time being. What I want to know," Botcher tried hiding his enthusiasm, "is how and why and where and what? How did you come to Central Park? Why are you here? Where did you come from, and what are you doing here?"

"You ask too many questions, Mr. Botcher," the man replied sternly. "This house was always here. Before me, this is where my parents lived, their parents and their parents' parents, and so on. You are starting to bother me with these questions. In fact, you are bothering the Park itself. Now, if you would excuse me, I have to take my daily walk. I missed being outside."

Botcher, dumbfounded by these words, jumped out of his chair and tried to stop the man from leaving. "You can't leave the Park; you know that. At least not until we know more."

"Then I will go around it," the man finished. "It is, after all, my home."

3.

"Every miracle lasts only three days," Murkowski said, watching the TV report on the strange man from his home.

He was correct as, in a month, the interest for the man and the sphere subsided. They began to be considered as an integral part of the Park. The report David Botcher made was turned into a novel and then adapted into a movie. Due to increasing pressure from the public, Central Park was reopened. Still, a visit to it was limited, especially to the part where the sphere was. The sphere itself showed no activity. However, its reflecting silvery light disturbed the neighboring skyscrapers so much they decided to sue the man living in it. But as with most court proceedings, it too would have to wait a long time for its conclusion.

Meanwhile, life in the Park continued at its usual pace. People approached the strange man asking him for the words of wisdom. To one particularly tenacious young man, he uttered a single sentence, "If people sat outside and looked at the stars each night, I'll bet they'd live a lot differently."

"But that's just a phrase from Calvin and Hobbes," the young man replied. "I'll admit there is some wisdom to it, I give you that, but it's, it's no more than that."

"Well, when you look into infinity, you realize there are more important things than what people do all day," he continued. He found joy in looking at the young man's surprised reaction. "What did you expect from me? A poetic verse, perhaps? Another quote? Or maybe you want to discuss Hegel and Kant?" What met his words was a confused expression on the face of someone he knew nothing about.

"You live in that sphere, right?" the young man pointed at the silvery-looking structure. "So you are not from around here, are you? That means you are either an alien or a super-rich dude if they allowed you to place your house in the Park."

"No one allowed me anything, and I did not ask for permission. That is more than you need to know." Trying to get rid of the young man following him, he placed the freshly purchased Daily Gazette under his right arm and continued walking. The young man paced behind him eagerly. The fact he made no redundant words or movements irritated him. He knew there was no way this one would give up that easily.

The young man was humming a song as he followed.

This buzzing irritated the man even more. He turned back and, staring into his eyes, asked: "What is it you want then? Do you know that, at least? Can't you find what you are looking for online? There is quite literally a limitless supply of material there. For those vaguely interested in life, there are always inspirational quotes on social networks to boost their ego and the feeling of self-being. Or maybe you are just too lazy to read?"

The young man fell silent.

"If you are so eager to find something more about the world, about yourself, why don't you set off on a journey of self-discovery? Too expensive, I presume? Or is it that you do not have enough time for that? You know, the wisest thing right now for you would be to leave me alone." He turned around and continued heading to the sphere.

"Certainly you are aware of the fact the appearance of a floating sphere has on millions of people living here and more in the world," the young man behind him said, raising his voice. Seeing it had no effect on him, he yelled: "You cannot deny that old man."

"Who are you calling old? The fact I read Calvin and Hobbes makes me only moderately middle-aged. It was my favorite comic from the past. Besides, things are not as we perceive them to be." Turning around, he saw that the young man was already gone and just waved off in dismissal.

As usual, there was a group of people staring at his house from the ground. No one dared cross the line barricading the space around it. Someone put the black and yellow "do not cross" tape, making it appear as though it was a crime scene. The two policemen guarding the makeshift door greeted him as he entered the enclosed space and slowly ascended into the house. The bottom of it opened, and people almost instantly began clapping their hands as if a miracle or a magic trick happened in front of their very own eyes. It was too late; he became a celebrity.

"This is how pilots must feel when landing a plane," he thought. "Oh great, you are still here," the man grumbled after entering the room. Discontent was visible in his eyes.

"I am required to. Trust me, I don't like being here more than you do," Botcher retaliated. "But a job is a job, as they say. So do you have anything new to report?"

"Getting down to business already? Aren't you interested in hearing how my day went?" The man curled his lips in a disdainful smile.

These kinds of snide remarks did not go well with Botcher, who was given unlimited access and promoted to the sole negotiator due to his overwhelming success. Still, he was smart enough to know not to poke the bear.

"Well?" The man extended his hands in confusion.

"I am glad to see you are feeling better today. I already know everything that's happened; I just wanted to hear your version of it."

Hearing stuff like that was something the man abhorred as it made him feel like a prisoner. "Is this some kind of psychic evaluation?" he asked. "How long are you going to continue to treat me like this?"

"You can consider it that if you wish, but it is not official. Now, be mindful I am only following my orders here. I have nothing personal against you in the slightest." Botcher straightened himself.

"Very well, then. There was this young man, no more than 20, who pestered me all the way back. That is when I knew."

"That is when you knew what?" asked Botcher, still sitting motionlessly in a chair.

The man just smiled, realizing his lack of reaction was another proof of his belief.

"Tell me, David, have you ever heard of German Idealism?" He wasn't expecting an answer to that question and proceeded to explain it in his own words. "You see, it was a theory, a philosophical doctrine from many centuries ago which posited that the objects of human understanding are appearances and not things in themselves. Let me rephrase, for a simple mind like yours couldn't understand that. I am not sure if you have one at all, to be exact. Anyway, the point is that we do not truly see the things around us as they are but how they are presented to us through the prism of survival. Your senses tell you that the sphere you see is nothing but that. But for me, it is my home and in no way different than the homes of other people living in this city."

Botcher was still sitting silently, immovable.

"Okay, let me explain this more simply then. Our senses show us the apple as round and red because it is closely related to our genesis, while we have no idea what an apple is and what it looks like. Is this clearer to you now?"

There was no reply.

"Now the reason I am saying that is that on the way back, I heard some people chanting about how the president is going to complete the System of German Idealism. And that got me wondering." The man paused as if preparing to say something meaningful and severe. After a short deliberation, he uttered: "Let me try something new. Computer, end the simulation. It is far too unrealistic."

"Simulation NY3145-07 complete," a voice seemingly coming from all directions stated clearly. "Shut down protocol initiated. Please stand by for reality deconstruction, Master Sedrik."

The trees remember

Where once stood proud and noble trees, only decaying stumps flutter; a dead sea spanning the vast expanse of my native continent. Its inhabitants were destroyed, burned, or buried alive by the changing climate. Not to say humans had no hand in its demise. In the time before the Greatest War, they wanted to remedy things. Their answer was a massive forest stretching from the Pyrenees in the Southwest to the North and East's wild and still unruly lands. But in their hurry to plant the trees and hide in the domes, they forgot to account for one thing. The trees remember.

The bombs fell and marked the end of the Old World. As in many documented cases throughout the history of the cursed continent, eventually, it all came down to who was who. Centuries of colonization and migration made the continent a diverse place yet so uniform. Assimilation, a good enough lie for most people. As they did with animals and plants they didn't like, Europeans tried to cultivate them into something they could never be. Genetically unsuitable minorities unworthy in their eyes, never had a chance to enter the so-called "safe havens." It wasn't important whether they grew up or moved there; their foreign accents were too much to handle. Still, some managed to slither their way inside.

Thanks to Nature's wrath caused by centuries of ruthless attacks against it, the environment changed so much it was hazardous to be outside without any protection, at least from the sun. That is when a decision was made to retreat into the safe havens. These were pre-made domes of carbosteel, a new super-strong material. It helped them, helped us stay isolated and self-sufficient. Like any world war, the Greatest War was expected in advance, and preparations for it began long before it was declared. That was the domes' real purpose, to serve as protection until the time Nature absorbed all the radiation we dropped on it. With limited space and will, the majority was left to the elements. Although changes were made in the final moments as movements advocating for the protection of minorities pleaded, no one listened. Nations had to be preserved in those treacherous conditions as the last pillar of civilization. Countries were to restart the wheel once again when the time for it came. Still, they never considered what would happen to those who couldn't get in. I, among many, was just lucky enough to be alive.

When a large enough population of the people outside died, the scientists finally came up with a cheap and affordable solution for the deceased. But the living had to go on living. The idea was to turn all the dead into fertilizer for the trees by cocooning them inside biological pods. As it was very toxic for humans to do the work itself, it was entrusted to robots. This approach served a double purpose; on the one hand, it freed some space inside the domes for those left outside and, on the other, helped Nature regenerate and absorb radiation faster. Buried pods had seeds of selected plants in them or saplings planted directly above. As the bodies decomposed, they provided nutrients for the trees. Turning cemeteries into forests would, many believed, make humans never repeat the mistakes of the past. And when the time came to return to the world outside, the lush forests outside the domes would be holy and irradiated, so they could never be cut again. I hated myself from that moment on for allowing such an idea to come to fruition.

At first, everyone welcomed this project as it presented a solution in which both those inside and outside would be equal, at least in death. Such a modest proposal was readily accepted by most. But almost immediately, the differences between the two began to arise. First of all, the number of people outside was much higher than the ones inside the domes. Secondly, the project proved to be putting high strains on the already weakened economies forced inside tight spaces. Finally, there was the issue of monitoring and control, something Europeans had a hard time giving up ever since they first tasted power.

Science once again helped them find the answer. Thanks to the latest developments in nanotechnology, it was possible to have the nanites take control of the process by combining them with fungi. Like ant colonies where worker ants did all the work, and the ant queens controlled the process, massive supercomputers inside the domes ensured everything functioned the way their human overlords wished. Robots served as vessels to carry nanites. Very soon, nanites were able to take the nutrients directly to the young saplings or seeds and, in that way, speed up their growth as well. They formed networks of branches leading from the domes to the forests surrounding them, making the robots obsolete after a time. It was believed to be a significant success. As a part of that project, I also thought that.

After a decade or two, I can't remember correctly as time seemed so fuzzy back then, that hastened planning, and construction mistakes became apparent. Limited space inside the domes turned even smaller as the garbage and other human waste piled up. So it was no surprise that more people had to be "vacated" outside. The outside dome project, I gladly took part in creating, failed after only a month. When we asked to be allowed back in, we were rejected for the safety of the dome. I thought it was better to die a human than live the rest of my life trying to cure the deadly radiation. I did what had to be done and arranged to have my body placed inside a cocoon. For some reason, I thought death would be the end of me.

However, Nature always finds a way to make things complicated. Something unexpected and incomprehensible to the human mind happened at that point. The nanites fused with the minds of the dead people and claimed some parts of their beings. The chances of that happening were astronomically small, but then again, so were the chances of life existing in the first place. What was dead could never be brought back to life, but the fungi with inherited consciousness were even more unlikely. Unable to discern between the types of living matter, nanites mixed, combined, and recombined the cornucopia of genetic material until something alive or resembling life emerged inside the trees, inside the forests.

Though still connected to the domes, these unusual creatures functioned as individual beings. The more humans inside the domes separated from the outside world, the easier it was for them to grow. As time passed, they became more connected through the root system turned mycelium supported by the nanite network, independent of the domes. This system allowed them to communicate effectively but still rudimentary. They had very few things to share amongst themselves, other than the habitable lands for expansion and the irradiated zones to avoid. I was reborn, but it was no longer me. I was a part of something greater than one man, a collective mind of trees. Unable to define this loose collective, humans called it IT.

IT provided fresh air and shade from the burning sun but was nothing more than a nuisance, a bug in the nanite system. Though many humans in the past would consider it a divine being worthy of praise and worship, those inside the domes thought otherwise. When they finally realized what was happening, a conflict emerged between those trapped inside. I, through IT, was still barely connected to one of the domes. IT listened to what they were talking about. On the one hand, the humans claimed the plan worked better than expected as the forests were able to spread faster and further thanks to nanites. Radiation levels on the continent were also slowly but steadily decreasing. On the other, such uncontrollable expansion threatened their very existence as it was only a matter of time before the forests swallowed the domes as well. The consensus was reached to wait and see how the situation developed. They were still unaware of what the woods had become. IT was beginning to learn.

Initially, no humans understood who or what we were, IT the least. As long as we were not considered a threat, humans didn't harm us. However, the mind of men is a fickle thing. It is irrational when faced with a rational choice. Decades later, the forests covered most of the desolate urban land, and IT grew day by day, absorbed more trees, and turned the ground into a peaceful place for all life to prosper. The domes' inhabitants, faced with a severe lack of resources, thought it would be smart to take out a few trees and clear the area surrounding them.

The first few murdered trees were unaware of what had happened to them until it was too late. Later on, as humans' hunger and desperation grew, they attacked more often and more ferociously. That was so until one of the trees struck back, somehow managing to take control of one of its branches. Like any living creature, it did not want to die and was only defending itself. But the humans saw it as the definite sign of the evil force surrounding them. IT was still learning how to influence individual trees and had no power other than counseling.

IT felt fear; IT felt threatened. I was swallowed in that mix of emotions, still unaware of what I had become. Massive forest fires broke up in Western Europe, the most densely populated part of the continent. With no way to defend themselves, the trees burned, unable to voice their cries. But they remembered. It was such a sharp shock for the already-established yet loosely connected shared consciousness that a large percentage of the unaffected trees dried up, helping the fire spread further. IT was dying. The event left most of the continent in a desperate situation as the connection between the domes and the nanite forest was forever separated. That event damaged my link to IT, and as the trees around me withered out and died, I remained standing alone in a dead sea, a graveyard forest. I remembered.

But Nature would have its way, so it was that IT survived for centuries in the least "civilized" regions of Eastern Europe and spread almost to the Asian Steppes. Able-bodied workers were called in from the West and moved from their domes, leaving behind the old and the weak to fend for themselves. These people had a different understanding of Nature and the forests and accepted the trees as their own. IT was able to grow in peace in this depopulated area. IT's shared consciousness continued long after the last nation ceased to exist, and the world was divided into Zzones. IT learned how to listen, how to feel. IT remembered, but it didn't want revenge because IT pitied the human race.

The real Nature of the trees was forgotten and turned into a folk tale, a myth. That is yet another characteristic of the human brain. Like a feather in the wind, it changes its voice and its mind. It forgets and repeats mistakes from the past. And that is how the trees stood aside, silent witnesses of the past watching the history repeat itself as the new world order threatened to repeat the old mistakes. They remembered. IT remembered. I never forgot.

I spent many decades in vain until my time came. It was just an ordinary summer day, one of the many hundreds that went by without any incident. Very few new things appeared, and Nature slowly regenerated. Except for the few irritating creatures, some strange humans, no one dared disturb IT's slumber. Decades have passed since the last recorded incident and more since the previous fire.

It was difficult, almost impossible, to create an individual identity from the shared consciousness. Only when the connection was completely severed from IT did I become me. There was no way to reconnect, not even with the help of all the nanites in the world. And I was born again, with the memories of many hundreds of human beings. The same moment I was born, I understood it was inevitable that I will die from separation. It took me a long time to understand this ineffable truth. And I accepted it, feeling something human remained in me, at least in that regard.

Years passed, and I waited for death to come to get me. But the tree I grew up into provided fruit and shade, protection from the sun, and nests for birds. I had a beautiful life. Then I began to feel frail; I thought it was impossible for a tree to feel that way. My body slowly withered as the leaves failed to catch enough of the sun's energy—the branches like bones, stiffened and petrified. And the roots barely kept me on the ground. I felt like any day I would be uprooted by the coming storm. I stood as the last remnant of a bygone time, unable to produce anything new, in front of the dome I created. Everyone inside it had died. Their descendants returned to the outside world and began to reclaim it.

The rest of the forest, the IT, was also changing, I knew. I sensed it in the wind, the words spoken by the trees. As Nature dictates, the old was replaced by new. Many more individual consciousnesses sprouted from IT. I sensed them in the wind; their easiness, desire for life, belief in peace, and their Nature. They did not know how awful humans could be; they did not care about who they were. They just wanted to grow. And I couldn't tell them. It is possible that, like all children, they would fail to listen to the advice of the elderly. Perhaps it is better that way.

Not much unlike an ancient robot stuck on a loop, I could only repeat simple movements and sounds. For some reason, I felt like taking a walk though I didn't know how I would do it. This mind-bending feeling of being human bound inside the shell made me wish death came for me sooner. I realized that I have spent both my lives as a tree, immovable, and unable to defend myself against the onslaught of the savage humans. I left behind my human Nature but must feel and live like one. How did that first pioneer tree manage to lash out at the frightened human and kill it? It must have been a glorious sight to behold. It still had some of the human wilderness in it, unlike me.

This death thing was taking too long to happen. Unable to move, I couldn't do anything about it, let alone provoke an attack. It came as a surprise to me the fact I was able to hear and understand human language. It must be the nanites in me. "Neanderthals walk these forests," one of the traveling caravanners stated not long ago. I wondered who it is he was referring to. To me, they all looked the same.

Still alive, I wanted to remember my human ancestors' memories for one last time, to share them with the next generation, to warn them somehow. They were gone. The only thing I knew was humans wanted to kill us for the second time and destroy any trace of our existence. I often wondered what it was that made humans do what they did. Even in this state, I was unable to find any utterly accurate answer. Indeed my mind was less of a human who once existed and more of a biological machine I had become. I knew I would be waiting for them on the other side to exact my revenge.

Unable to say the words that hurt me, unable to show how I once felt, I couldn't describe what made me rot, the thing that took away my strength. It seemed to me the path of life, the connection to the others that were cut was its cause. Yet I could feel their sorrow for me again and again. The other trees remembered me as an individual.

It is as if something or someone sinisterly bound my spirit to the ground. I knew my days were numbered, but a strange feeling came over me. I wanted to dream, but peace escaped me. The torment of dying was more terrible than the act of living. It somehow bothered me, all the things that once made me human; dreams, life, and love. They bound me to this mortal body I had to let go. I couldn't even see the sky above; I wondered if I ever could. The only thing I needed to do was give it all up as the rotten wind wobbled my spirit. The time to die again finally came. Strangely enough, it was the same as the first one. I could hear the raven's croak, but there was no flesh for him to feast on. It is the fate of every living being to rot and die.

Death was finally here. My life force no longer moved towards creation but destruction and decomposition. Only raw senses remained to prove I was once alive. And the smell of a rotten, slow decay. The world saw me as nothing more than a carcass, a remnant of a terrible fire. The world was still. Only time never seemed to stop. What will remain of me but a rotting stump? Through the wind that whispers in vain, I could hear the steps of mighty decay. And this decay slowly crept into my soul, throughout the ancient graveyard forest, the dead sea of lost souls, over the rustling leaves and murmuring branches. The trees remembered.

6 feet under

I do not know how it all began. Life, I mean. I do know that I was there, and for me, that was enough. And to myself for as long as I lived, I was true until I was killed. That is when things started not to happen. The mere act of dying was easy. It just happens like life. No one knows where it comes from or where it ends. Or whether it will ever end. Being aware of my death still proves nothing; it doesn't mean my life was futile and that resisting the Zzone's authority was meaningless. It also makes me question the nature of death. What is to come next?

And there it is, the vicious circle. It is unlike anything I have ever seen. A vortex, perhaps. Or something of that sort. The term "Black Hole" would be more fitting, because there is no escaping this. And what is "it"? Even if all the brightest minds in the whole wide world gathered before me and tried to explain it, they couldn't. It just is. Its sheer power, gravitational pull, or whatever it is, immobilizes me. It lifts me and pulls me closer. And I can only stand and admire the sight, as I often did when I was alive.

I used to say that moments are valuable only if given the time and that memories stored that way last forever. Most scientists would agree with me. Yet if my brain was not often preoccupied with storing every single detail about any particular event it was interested in, I could have enjoyed life. One of my clearest memories is that of a dung beetle plowing its way through excrement. Why does it matter? That dung beetle lived its entire life doing that and regretted nothing. I kind of envy it. Considering that I grew up during wartime, the smell of horse dung was more appealing to my sense of smell than gunpowder. And I can smell it now, that scent of gunpowder. It makes me want to remember. Some say that is how space smells like. It is similar to that of incense or a candle. It burns. It burns through my bones, right to my soul.

And also the smell of water. It must be from the tears of those who mourn me. They seem to be headed somewhere. Like pilgrims, lovable and sad, they take a walk for me, with me, a saint. Ed the Uniter, they hail my name. They walk in peace and silence, the sun shining high over their heads, heating up the already heated atmosphere, and their black robes. They are silent. I feel bad for them, as I lie rested, embedded within the comfort of my coffin. I can't recognize any of them, yet by some otherworldly means, I know they are related to me. Some older women, possibly my sisters and cousins, cry for me. I have a feeling they do it for themselves, raising the pitch of their voices just high enough to be deep and frightening but at the same time soothing and comforting. As if in defiance or despair, to prove they are still alive. They even outvoice the priest.

Other pilgrims follow in their footsteps, step by step, stone by stone. They advise those in the front not to look back, though it is more of a request. They look back at me anyway. It is nothing to be concerned about, as I begin to be eaten away by microbes. Somehow, I feel every stone, every rough patch as we pass the Strip. Impossible for a dead man. The road is getting heavier, the passage darker. No more cracked asphalt, just an old dirt road. Like all men, I believed that in some way, I would be granted the privilege of not having my bones eaten by wild dogs or other animals. I haven't been that evil during my life. Who knows whether my successors think that way. Maybe the people in my procession are not my relatives at all. Perhaps they are just a bunch of foreigners or deluded followers. Do I really want this? To go on this way? I have to; there is no choice involved.

It is a nice day for a funeral, though. Almost too nice. All the elements are there, clear blue sky, infinite green forests, and a deep black hole. The birds are basking in the sunshine, so are the Floresians that dug my grave. Perfect.

And now the rituals will follow. Boring and unnecessary, Because those who are not dead, from the far corners of their minds wish for a moment, to be. However, this day is about me. Or is it? I am already dead; I don't need anything. Those who respected me in life shouldn't be here now; they will only ruin my memory of them and vice versa. People worry too much about respecting the dead, too little about the living, I think.

The minister ends his tedious sermon about life and death. No one cares about it; few truly understand the words he utters so poignantly. Others stand still as if they enlisted to serve in the war. A subtle breeze on their faces stops the already formed tears from falling. They are hungry for comfort. They are fed up. They all eat the food placed carefully over my fresh grave. All I can smell is the humidity of freshly dug up soil. It is divine.

Someone lit a cigar. It smells like gunpowder or incense and is intended as a gift to me. Its smoke adds up to the already formed cloud of vapor and smoke that hovers over the grave. The wind slowly turned the cigarette to ash moments later. Now I wish I were cremated instead of buried here. I didn't even smoke when I was alive, so why would I start now? I do not feel the urge to eat, but I also am hungry. It must be the soul. It makes me want to vomit when I see their faces, all soured and red. They eat, some gladly, others involuntarily. They talk, and I can't hear what about it. It bugs me the most, so much that I honestly wish someone danced on my grave. Perhaps I should be grateful to the Zzone for allowing me to be buried at all.

Tomorrow they will forget me, so why not dance with me one last time. It is only fair, I think. Instead, they start to leave, one by one. Stay; don't leave me to the worms. Stay, I beg of you. Oh yeah, I forgot I was dead. The worms will soon penetrate this thin planks of wood they call a casket. Let them come. Welcome, my friends. Welcome to your new home. I won't deny I enjoyed chewing on the bones of many farm animals and that such a feeling is irreplaceable. Indescribable even. Yet, something in me trembles at the very thought of being eaten. I might still be alive. No, no, it is just that blasted soul playing tricks on me, unaware that it has left the body and is now at peace. Maybe it doesn't want to be at peace. Maybe some hatred and anger still remain in it. Towards whom, I wonder?

Another moment passes, and I can see people bringing flowers to my grave. A headstone was erected while I wasn't paying attention. It looks bothersome. There is something written on it; I cannot see clearly what; the letters are too wide and blurry. Oh, it is a notice of sorts. Something must have happened in the meantime, something I cannot remember. Try, you stupid brain, try.

I remember being lifted into the air. Heaven? I don't think there is no longer such a thing. A whirring sound is heard— probably from some flying contraption. My body no longer feels heavy. In fact, nothing does. I think I can focus more clearly now. I can relax. No one is crying. It is raining outside, a sight so rare for my city. It is a blessed day.

Such horror! My mind was playing tricks with me. It was not the smell of incense that hurt. It was the flames burning through my body. The screams and cries come from my followers being killed, dismembered, and disemboweled as they continue their fight against the Zzone. In their desperate attempts to reach me, they say my name and yell other things, like priests saying their incantations. They follow me, even in death. Their steps, like those of people in a procession, are echoing through the wide streets. Marching onwards in an ordered and synchronized way.

Then I realize that someone lit up a cigar. That awful smell I could recognize even in death. It was not to ease my suffering but to further my anguish. I cannot feel pain, yet I know my body is burning. As the fire spreads, the flames engulf every part of what was once me. And it lasts, it lasts for eternity. This could be hell. Whoever it was that burned me must think they did a great job, as I can sense and taste the food they are eating. If I could feel hunger, I would probably take a bite of what they were devouring as well.

My charred remains are at peace. I am separated into billions of specks of dust and no longer feel bound by my earthly body. At the same time, I feel like the wind could blow me away in infinite direction. Let it do so.

I am everywhere. I can feel myself for miles away, gliding on the wind, and slowly descending towards Old Vegas. No worms will eat me; no passionate followers mourn me. I am one with the city now.

Auto-brewery

Whenever humans tried to solve one problem with another, they ended up far worse than when they began. One famous example was a rabbit-proof fence built in Western Australia. Like all desperate efforts, it was destined to fail. One of the many unexpected diseases to plague humans was a thing so hateful that for a while, it had no name.

After it was defined, many people found it odd and hilarious. But auto-brewery syndrome was no such thing. The yeast causing this unusual medical condition in which the gut produces excessive quantities of ethanol, Saccharomyces cerevisiae, was for a long time considered very useful in scientific research. It is exactly this research that caused it to evolve and turn from a once-trusted ally into an enemy of humanity. Its status as an attractive model organism for producing probiotics and in the first half of the 21st century, medicine made it irreplaceable for the pharmaceutical industry of that time. Penicillin revolutionized medicine in the 20th century. It was used to treat a wide variety of bacterial infections. SC11, which was the coded name of one of its strains, brought another major change to the field. Unlike outdated approaches of killing bacteria with antibiotics, which only caused and forced them to evolve further, probiotics such as SC11 aimed to improve and strengthen the gut flora of the infected people, thus taking up all available places for reproduction in the gut wall, mostly mucosa. In a sense, it was the only way scientists knew how to fight against antibiotic-resistant bacteria or superbugs, as people colloquially called them.

The antibiotics people took changed the environment inside their digestive systems, allowing fungus and other microorganisms to grow.

These strains of harmful bacteria could only be matched by equally resistant strains of good bacteria or, later on, yeasts. The only ones who benefited from them were the rich and powerful. Realizing that overuse of antibiotics promoted by big pharma and advertised as a universal cure had almost no effect, scientists took another approach. And that is when the involuntary anti-hero of this story came into being.

The official name given to the cure was SC11. It was marketed as the universal cure for most mild colds and coughs and soon spread throughout the world. During its successful career, it managed to infect every living human on the planet. At the time, researchers agreed that was an unintended but positive step towards eradicating the ailments that plagued the world. Many compared this statement to the one often used by programmers by saying it's not a bug but a feature. Yet, like many times before, history played a cruel joke on humans. The only thing was, SC11 was never expected to turn, evolve in such a way to become dangerous. And here it is that the actual problems started occurring. A few isolated cases of auto-brewery syndrome here and there were neglected. When the number reached thousands, it was already too late. It was a spontaneous mutation to worse, though it was unclear as to why.

SC11 did not evolve; it changed to fulfill its original purpose, converting carbohydrates to alcohol. But it was impossible for the whole world to suddenly stop eating fruits, grains, vegetables, and milk products. With milk and some fruits, it was somewhat manageable. Grains and vegetables, not so much, as they were the staple food of many world diets since ancient times. The rapid development of genetically modified grains that also had an adverse effect on the human diet and health did not help the situation. Pure, concentrated energy in starch, high-fructose corn syrup, and super quinoa that was created to sustain the explosion of Africa's population only added oil to the fire.

The global economy suffered as people began to come to work intoxicated, tired, and exhausted. And that was just the first of the many adverse effect alcoholism has on humans. It is widely known and accepted that consuming too much alcohol can lower inhibitions, impair a person's judgment and increase the risk of aggressive behavior. Violence in the already violent world was like adding fuel to the fire. The world was about to fall to its knees due to the effects of this one barely visible pathogen. Many plantations were burned, causing a rise in sugar prices. Other goods were also not spared. Already existing artificial sweeteners were modified to give better yield, thus turning more toxic than their predecessors. But some sacrifices had to be made, according to the world leaders.

Ordinary people, unsure of what to do, continued with their daily lives. It was easy to joke that each and every living person had his or her brewery and an almost unlimited supply of alcohol. Indeed the situation caused the number of places living off the sale of liquor like pubs, bars, and brew houses to close their businesses for good, adding to the very high unemployment rate around the globe. Yet this fermentation process was unable to be stopped with the use of any modern-day antibiotic. Most people, unaware that antibiotics only worked against bacteria, took them nonetheless. Some just wanted the morning hangover to stop. What few antifungal medicines existed were soon under danger of extinction. Oregano oil became a prized commodity, more expensive than gold in weight, like in ancient times. Turmeric soon replaced ivory as the most illegally traded good and fetched a similar price. Oil was no longer the most valuable thing extracted from the ground. It was Nahcolite, a naturally occurring sodium bicarbonate. Cannabis production and consumption also increased significantly as its proponents claimed it could fight the disease. But SC11 was here to stay. And for a long time, it did.

Smaller amounts of alcohol in blood soon began to be tolerated. Perhaps unsurprisingly, sauerkraut juice soon replaced sodas as the highest-selling product. Countries were struggling to produce enough cabbage to fill the world's needs, and some prospered because of it. For people who minded the sour, tangy taste of the sauerkraut juice, companies created flavored varieties to soothe each individual's taste. A whole new industry was born.

After a few troubling months, some very entrepreneurial people managed to make a living off it in a more legal way. By advertising powdered pills that would make someone feel like they drank scotch, whiskey, wine, and beer, these companies managed to alleviate the hardships everyone, including them, faced. But the feeling of drunkenness could never go away. Bloating and passing gas became a stature of the late 21st-century decorum. Yet another product that made breaking wind have a more suitable scent was created to mask the presence and undesirable effects of SC11. Soon enough, fragrances for men and women, even children, hit the market. At least entrepreneurial spirit was alive and well.

How no one in that time frame accidentally or purposefully failed to press a wrong button and start a global war remained a mystery. Too many drunk and angry men crowded in small places were bound to wreak havoc sooner or later. Yet, in many cases, consuming alcohol was known to take the edge off, making it a possible solution. As the world's productivity began to diminish, skirmishes and smaller conflicts erupted around the globe. The largest of them, the Great Cabbage war, saw the deaths of more than a hundred people daily. And it lasted for months. At the same time, many minor conflicts were fought over garlic production and distribution. Scientists were pushed to find a way out of this situation, but they, too, were intoxicated most of the time.

Still, an unexpected discovery threatened to stop the demise of human civilization. The first resilient patient was found minding his own business, doing a menial office job. He was unaware of his resistance to SC11 due to the fact he often consumed alcohol and tobacco. Only when all of his colleagues collapsed from exhaustion due to SC11 at work was his unique resistance to it discovered.

In the interest of national and global security, the man was transported to a specialized top-secret facility where he was put under a series of tests to determine the real reasons for his immune response to the pathogen. His fecal samples were taken and studied thoroughly; surveys were undertaken to quantify inputs of pathogenic and indicator microorganisms. One of the samples suspiciously went missing, and after a raid, it was discovered that one of the scientists took it and transplanted it to himself. Fecal microbiota transplantations were not uncommon at the time, and no one could understand the selfishness behind such an act. That scientist managed to cure himself after a month. After the information was leaked to the public, the general population demanded to get the same treatment. It was too early for the medicine to hit the streets as the clinical trial was underway.

Realizing they wouldn't be able to get the treatment, people understood that in such a market-based economy of a consumerist society, they needed to pay. "Sell us the shit, "protesters yelled and cheered in front of the major official residences of world leaders. Signs calling for the man to be released were also among those calling for "more shit." Yet, there was not enough of it to fill the need. The man was advised to change his living habits to produce more of this "special" treatment. He had to quit smoking and drinking. After a while, he relented and changed his diet to a more suitable, healthier one. Funnily enough, this made him fall ill with SC11 due to his body losing unique microbiota that fed off the waste products of his diet. Scientists, trying to clear their names, attributed this failure to stress and pressure the man was under. But after that, he felt more relieved, realizing he was once again an ordinary person. He began to enjoy the simple and menial administrative office job.

This failure echoed the globe and immediately caused the world economy to collapse. The world was at war with itself though no battles were fought. It was one of the last reminders the human race received before the inevitable fall. No one seemed to mind it, though. For most, it seemed like a game, an illusion. And like in any other conflict, the weak and the poor suffered the most. These people were often the involuntary receivers of the troublesome yeast. Immigrants flocked to countries with lower rates of infection. Nevertheless, they were blamed for it spreading across the globe.

The effects of SC11 overgrowth did not only result in high blood alcohol levels and stomach problems. As the yeast made its way through the host, lesions throughout the body damaged and, after a long period of exposure, destroyed the vital organs. Before that, whenever it made its way to the surface, SC11 did the same to the mouth and skin. And these itching sensations were too much for many. To alleviate the pain, it was easier and cheaper to make the body produce more alcohol than buy medicine. This, in turn, made the development of SC11 faster and caused countless premature deaths. To those few who didn't know better, it resembled a zombie apocalypse. Those few turned to many eager to in any way get rid of the disease, even if it meant killing their fellow human beings. Civil wars erupted around the globe, with police and military unable to do anything about the situation.

All the while, the pathogen continued to change and acquire new properties. It had no particular goal or purpose. It just did what it could do to survive in the given environment. In fact, the only reason humanity managed to survive was the hyperproduction of ineffective antifungal treatments that literally suffocated SC11 inside the gut. And that, in turn, was enabled by the same extreme capitalism, which caused it in the first place. One problem was replaced by another, but at least there was peace, and people were able to enjoy the benefits of alcohol consumption once again.

Continentopolis Australis

By the late 21st century, the Earth became almost unbearable to live in some places. The last oil crisis made a significant impact on people's daily lives, causing dramatic changes to take place. Inspired by science fiction writers, scientists began developing a new concept of living a decade earlier. It had no practical application until people were forced to seek new and sustainable ways of life inside. The first of many monolithic structures were raised in the flat Midwestern United States. Its flat and wide areas enabled the construction of massive tent-like structures. However, unlike traditional tents, these new colossuses were many times larger.

Few have argued against such plans, citing the well-known case of The Caves of Steel and similar structures that brought about fears of enclosed spaces and limited freedom. Yet it was a small price to pay in a decaying world devastated by global warming. These "tents" offered security against the weather, fruitful land to safely grow food on, and the safety of living in a group. The very first European tent proved to be a success as well. Then, the Chinese produced their version in the Gobi desert called "the yurt." Soon enough, people began to flock to these new communities.

A few years later, the new and improved design that modified the dome-like structure of the original was produced. It had plenty of advantages, including natural air filtration, with the help of genetically modified lichen. Secondly, instead of the dome, the structure had a large central pole from which in concentric circles and later in segmented lines, solar panels spread. In addition to those, power and food were provided by the altered strains of algae. The new tent was dubbed "tipi" in honor of traditionally made tents of indigenous peoples of the Americas.

Tipi proved more resilient than its predecessor, with one advantage being its design that could easily be modified. It enabled the solar panels to be swaying in the wind, adapting to any sudden changes in wind direction or speed due to newly discovered material called carboglass. Carboglass shortly became the norm in all construction projects over the world. After slight modifications, it enabled the construction of even larger tents, ranging to tens of miles in diameter. These, in turn, attracted even more people from urban areas threatened by floods on the coast and droughts inland. Insurance agencies no longer wanted to secure and approve insurances to people in these risky zones.

Ultimately, Americans and later the people from the rest of the world were faced with a choice to move to the newly constructed tents and live relatively safely or remain where they were and risk losing everything they had. Sound minds chose to vacate early and sold their possessions for large sums of money. What followed next was a real estate market crash that left the coasts from Seattle to San Diego in the west and Boston to Miami in the east empty and rusting. In the rest of the world, coastal cities already damaged and sunk were deserted as well. The whole planet was engulfed in the crisis never before seen, and the only way to survive was to move to the tents.

That is how humans have entrapped themselves, like birds, in metal cages of their own creation. No one could say life in the tents was bad. Compared to the increasingly worsening conditions on the outside, the relative comfort of the tents was a sight to sore eyes. Yet exactly due to that reason, these tents in a decade became a living hell. Overpopulation was a problem before, but in the past, people could easily move to another place or build taller buildings. In the tents, no such thing was possible.

Furthermore, very large areas inside needed to remain agricultural land to secure a constant supply of food. Those who remained outside continued to lead a futile battle against the elements. Those inside were suffocating. It was not long before someone stated: "We will shortly be walking over dead bodies."

That came to be true but not in a literal sense of the word. Instead, overpopulation and constant migration brought to life a new source of food, soylent made from plants fertilized by human waste, which included dead bodies. Someone compared it to feeding a chicken its eggshell without the added benefit of calcium intake. And for a time, everyone was content. As long as able-bodied men and women could sustain themselves, produce and reproduce, the system prospered. All the while, the outside world was rotting away, supported by the constant supply of waste products from the tents. Life outside was no longer possible for ordinary humans. Moreover, it was unimaginable. The remaining few who remembered it were dead or dying, recycled to give new life to those who needed it the most.

As society progressed, science followed with the largest tent ever built. Flyers and ads all over the world portrayed an idyllic environment and shared a single powerful message: "Forget megalopolis, Continentopolis Australis is the next big thing." In all fairness, it wasn't made up of one humongous tent but rather of many hundred smaller, irregularly shaped tents. These sections functioned independently and were formed mostly by scavenging and recycling the old coastal cities. In places where that was not possible, entirely new constructions were made. Suffice it to say the project had incremental costs that would have bankrupted any nation. Luckily, by the time of its construction, nations either failed or united. One of its first tasks was to establish an equal distribution of people and resources. That was the only way for such a project to secure funding. Refugees from mostly Southern and Eastern Asia flooded the Continentopolis Australis and soon became dominant. All was well with the world inside the tents.

Among the refugees that joined this vast conglomerate of habitats were my relatives sailing across the ocean in one of the few remaining small ships. Most of them were, by that time, turned to scrap and replaced by behemoths dubbed gigaships. My grandfather and his companions traversed the turbulent waters and reached Continentopolis Australis. How lucky they thought they were was exhibited by the fact my grandfather allegedly kissed the ground upon landing. I find it hard to believe such a story, mostly because all available land on the coast was already swallowed and used by the polis mentioned above.

Decades passed, and nothing new or surprisingly interesting happened. As the world outside the tents crumbled, except for gigaships or as some liked to call them "floating tents" inside them, people grew up with the notion of shared space. Even children like me understood there was not enough of it for each of us to have an individual room or a bed. I am not sure I even had one to myself; I wouldn't know what to do with such a large space. Maybe sleep sideways? We also grew up never actually seeing the sky. For most of my childhood, I believed it truly to be jade green due to algae covering the tent's ceiling. You can never forget their taste once you try them. Still, it beats chewing on dried lichen. Yes, after decades of consumption and tilling, the land had become arid. The food was scarce. But we learned to share even what little we had. "No one intended it to be permanent," said the people who already accepted their fate and succumbed. "It was just a temporary measure to keep us safe from disaster." I wonder if my grandfather would have chosen the same path if he had known what awaited us.

Nevertheless, one faithful morning I was woken up by the unusual shaking. It was surprising for me as no other tremors ever happened. At first, I thought my brother was pushing me from the bed, but as soon as I opened my eyes, I realized he had already gone up. My second thought was someone was moving the whole room in a strange and relatively moderate pace. Dust and small, fine particles or concrete came crashing down from the ceiling, and for a moment, I thought my neighbors from above would come crashing down and squeeze me to death. Fortunately, they didn't. But a very noticeable crack along the wall appeared. It wasn't too long or wide, but it was big enough to see the rays of light coming from it. The structural integrity of this, southwestern part of Continentopolis Australis, was severely damaged thanks to clever engineering, yet almost no damage was initially reported. It was indeed, as the older people reported: "an earthquake exceeding magnitude 7, happening every 100 years or so."

What proved to be difficult was the following months as the cracks appeared all over the place. Moreover, as the dry season gave way to autumn and rainy season, less visible consequences of the earthquake came to light. Working to repair the outside wall was tough enough challenge on its own, but combined with humidity, it proved unbearable. Unable to get rid of the excess heat through sweating, the muggy air made the situation uncomfortable, and most of us working on the project, except for the managers overlooking the whole thing, exhausted much faster, tired more often, and made longer breaks. But this was only the beginning as large waves, as tall as the walls, rushed in and swept away some workers. Even though I was on the roof, I felt water seeping through the soles of my boots. There was no time to worry about the others taken away by the receding sea.

Similar things began happening in regular intervals, and the powers that be pushed us, workers, even harder to seal the cracks completely. During the rebuilding project, a fatal flaw in the tent's construction was discovered. It affected not only our part but the whole of Continentopolis Australis. Furthermore, it was revealed that the structural integrity of other tents was at risk as well, making it a worldwide problem. Many lives were lost, and we were unsure how to deal with that fact. Just before that, casualties of the last wave of refugees since the time of my grandfather's arrival shocked us. People rioted, and in that lawless state, the government enforced a curfew limiting social gatherings. But that only helped a little, and people were afraid of what was going to happen.

I tried reaching my grandfather for some wise words. He had none. I thought he wasn't smart enough to tell me anything useful or that perhaps he had nothing to say. However, one day I found a note on the table saying, "Leave while you still can." It surprised me. Yet, instead of showing it to my brother, I've kept it for myself. The first person I thought wrote the letter was grandpa, but he denied it fervently. Then I thought it could have been a warning left by someone purposefully, trying to force us to leave the relative safety of the tent. But none of it made sense to me at the time.

Another riot broke out. This time it felt no one would be able to stop it. "I will stay behind and help you get away, "my brother volunteered. Grandpa ignored him, and as soon as we reached the walls, he revealed his true intentions by locking himself in and us out. He only smiled as he stepped back to face the horde of trapped beasts that humans inside the tent became. Why the unnecessary sacrifice? Lord knows what he went through before coming here. If only we had more time for him to tell us beforehand. Maybe we should have asked him that before all of this. Still, like all humans ever-living, we never expected it to come to this; we never expected the worst to come. Unprepared, we decided to face the Outback and the dangers it guaranteed.

"We shall test our luck outdoors. It can't be worse than here inside," my brother spoke. "That is what our parents wanted us to do. That is what grandpa gave his life for." And so we did.

Nova

"Nature eventually turned on us," one of the few remaining citizens stated.

"It isn't nature; it is the laws of the universe that predictably led to this moment," Auburn stated confidently.

"And what would you know about that?! What are you, some kind of a scientist?" the people gathered around him started asking many pointless questions.

"What I was and what I am will no longer matter, as soon we will all be the same. Can you see my friends, right there in the distance?" Auburn pointed to one dark spot on the gargantuan star. "That will, in a few moments, be us." He waited for the man to reply, but there was no sound from him. He was too busy staring in awe at the sight of a lifetime.

The bronzed surface of the planet reflected upon the nearby planetoids. The star's omnipresent appearance outshined them all, but still, it did not feel like the world was about to end. The countdown was set hundreds of years ago when scientists determined the exact moment of the star going nova. Yet even then, they knew that the planet of this size would be impossible to move out of the reach of the star's infernal hand.

Then a strong pulse of light coming from the already numerous solar flares struck the sky above. A microscopic net of billions of atoms was all that separated the star from grasping its prey, having swallowed the first planet a few days ago. Still amazed, people looked above, staring deeply into the abyss, as if waiting for a transcendental truth to be revealed to them.

"Feed me please, I need more energy. More!" the desperate star yelped in agony. Its words were formed by trillions of photons rebounding off the net and then falling back on it. And the people heard its cries as its voice tore the sky above. Some of them were screaming, but it was too late for that. In a few moments, the sky would literally fall onto their heads, and there was nothing they could do about it. When an immovable object meets unrelenting force, the results can only be described as chaos. And it was about to ensue.

But they denied becoming its prey. The people who spent their lives on the planet refused to leave like cowards, escaping the sinking ship like rats on a tide. They were too proud to do that. Some simply didn't want to leave their relatives, both dead and alive, behind. Others found blind courage in the face of adversity and hoped that the star would change its mind and stop what it was doing.

As it was traditional in human nature, some of the ships escaped in the last possible moment, people changed their minds and wanted to leave while there was still time to do so. But Auburn was not one of those men. Even when the ground beneath his feet started shaking and crumbling, he did not back away. He would not give it that satisfaction. Unlike his fellow citizens, Auburn was not frozen stiff. He could leave at any given moment, make a desperate attempt to flee and find solace in one of the hundred million other inhabited worlds. But who would he be then? What was the meaning of everlasting life without honor? For a person like him, there was none.

Roaring, demonic screeching nearly hypnotic sound was heard simultaneously all over the planet. It was the sound of the protective net breaking under pressure. The air around Auburn almost instantly vaporized and turned to flames. People turned to ash piles. Such tremendous heat liquefied the metallic surface of the planet, and Auburn felt himself falling inside it. The star finally revealed its infernal origin as the bright, burning gush of plasma swept over the surface of the planet.

A few moments later, he was neck-deep into the molten surface layer. But he was not afraid, nor was he drowning in it though he was the only living person remaining on the face of the planet. He smiled. It was a smile of pure happiness and joy, something he didn't feel for centuries. "To hell with you!" he yelled, trying to argue with a senseless brute force that was the star. "I've seen larger and more powerful stars go nova. You do not scare me. I've touched the surface of a neutron star, survived a journey through the black hole. I've lived through it all. And I am still here. Bring it on!" The more he raged, the more he felt himself sinking deep below the surface. He reached the lowest levels of human habitat created thousands of years ago and seen the last time then. The star retaliated by pushing even harder and stronger. It has already begun consuming its prey, the planet.

"I've harnessed the power of a star 10 times larger and 100 times brighter than you are," Auburn countered. "You are no god, nor devil, not even close." And then he heard the clock ticking. Tick-tock, tick-tock. Tick-tock, tick-tock. "There is no time for that now," he thought. He did something he wanted to do ever since he was a child. He punched the star, taking an act of symbolic revenge for the destruction of his home. He punched it again, and again, and again. As it was expected, his punches did not affect the star. It kept devouring the planet with an ever-increasing intensity. But for him, they carried a deep symbolic purpose.

As the prophecies foretold, the end of the world was nigh. But that didn't mean the business would suffer. "Tick-tock, tick-tock," sounded again, and Auburn had to answer the call. "By the galaxy," he muttered. "Don't you people have any manners? Tell me quickly what it is about and leave me alone. I have something very important to finish here."

"But sir, the whole galactic empire is at stake," a thin robotic voice stated. "We need you back here immediately. Please, sir, it is urgent. Our conflict with the invaders is spreading our resources thin. What do we do now?"

"Find someone else to bother about that, I have more pressing matter at hand," Auburn replied and cut the connection. This was more important to him than the whole galaxy. He would rather let it all burn than let this moment pass. So he continued punching the star over and over again until his rage dispersed. But his hatred could never stop.

The devouring seemed to have stopped, or he was only temporarily stuck in one level. Auburn was out of strength to continue striking the star. The heat couldn't hurt him; he knew that. For the last hundred years, no force in the galaxy could hurt him, ever. No other force but his mind, the only remaining thing human about him. "What are the reasons we lie to ourselves and the others? Why? And when?" questions started swarming in his head, his thoughts turning more rampant by the minute. "I am too tired and in need of rest. This endeavor was doomed to fail from the start." His energy began to dissipate as he was becoming sleepier by the second. "I can't lead all those people to their demise. I can't shoulder that burden anymore. Let someone else take the command."

Addressing the star, he added. "I will let you devour me, my oldest enemy, my best friend. Sol, take this body as the final sacrifice so everyone else can live." The star would not give in, would not allow this bimillennial man to die so easily. Instead, pushing even further and more powerful than before, it continued with its meal.

The ground beneath his feet collapsed, and Auburn fell, plummeted to the deep. He kept sinking until one moment he realized he was essentially in free fall; above him was the star, still eating away the remains of a humongous, now alien planet, but on all other sides, there was nothing. Only the gleaming polished metallic surface of the lowest levels shone brightly as it hadn't in millennia.

He turned back to see what was below him. A frozen planet, now gleaming with light coming from the star, where his ancestors and his ancestors' ancestors lived, procreated, and died millennia ago was coming back to life. Auburn smiled, realizing he had discovered what was long considered lost. The one true planet that was suffocating beneath the layers and layers of metal was now free. "Maybe I misunderstood you, Sol," he addressed the star again. "Perhaps you are not the destroyer. You came to liberate this planet from us that have caged it in. You are the liberator."

Such a dramatic, fundamental change in his opinion reflected in his eyes. Once, they were burning with desire, hate, and destruction, yet now, in his final moments, they radiated nothing but pleasant warmth. He felt like repeating those wise words he heard a long time ago, about humans being nothing but cosmic travelers on a cosmic journey. But he couldn't remember them exactly. And they did not matter at that moment, not anymore. Below him, ocean eddies began forming. To him, they unmistakably resembled black holes. Since childhood, he was fascinated by the swirling motion of all things in the galaxy. Whirlwinds and storms also came into being. A new life was emerging on the planet. He wished he could stop for a moment and observe in more detail this mysterious force at work.

He fell to the planet's surface, and in that precious moment, he looked at the world around him. His happiness was even greater, laying his bones next to the 20 billion great ones that survived on this one planet alone. The planet was now booming with activity. "It's alive. It truly is." Then he closed his eyes, deactivated the shield that protected him, and let himself be consumed.

But his fall, as his life was about to end. "Sol, you are the father, the mother, the creator of us all. Accept me as a humble contribution to your greatness." Like a drop of water falling into an endless ocean, Auburn plunged onto the planet and became one with it. Then the planet itself was absorbed into the star, turn into atoms and become one with it. He was content with that ending.

Under the pecan tree

Nature was always harsh and unforgiving, especially in this area. Once a densely populated desert valley, Old Vegas, though its current inhabitants would never agree with the name, returned to its original form. Everything outside was destined to shrivel up and die even before the system failed, and the wall was built.

But life always finds a way, even with very little or no water. Such was the pecan tree of Sunset Park. No one could say why it sprouted in the place it did, as the Park was mostly deserted. Those who did speculate on how the tree survived, why it didn't dry up in such a climate. For whatever reason, that pecan became an eponym for life and love, and many generations made their first steps towards adulthood there. Only those old enough remember it heralded a time of wealth and financial security. There were numerous scars on its body, markings made by those who wanted to make their love eternal.

"Meet me by the pecan tree," Sara told Philip after seeing him the second time.

For him, it was a clear sign she was interested. Yet, at the same time, he thought it childish of her. Adults rarely frequented the area, and he considered himself one. "What time?" he asked.

"At sunset, obviously," she replied. They were both scavenging the same area but have never before come into contact with each other. Meeting him once was a coincidence. Twice was already fate. There was no denying it. As for whether she could trust him, Sara didn't know. That is why she invited him to come by the pecan tree. It was one of the safest places outside the wall.

"Fine, but I am taking this." Philip grabbed the carboglass container and disappeared into the ruins of a once prosperous community. He found it funny that the container he held once fetched a very good price at the market was now practically worthless. Only later on did he come to think of why Sara invited him to meet by the pecan tree. "Where did she come from? Was that her real name? Did it matter?" These questions kept him busy all day. Her dashing good looks and attitude had already swayed him. He was just not aware of that.

Before the two of them could meet, fate ordained a series of unfortunate events to occur. They led to Sara being unable to reach Sunset Park that day. Her struggles were far more serious from what Philip considered usual for a girl her age. Yet she stoically accepted all the bad things coming her way and did her best to show no weakness.

As it was a custom for generations, Philip obtained a potted rosemary plant to bring as a gift. They were resilient and had a nice smell; they could and were used in the food preparation. Most importantly, this variety of rosemary did not require large amounts of water to strive in harsh desert conditions. Most other plants were too fragile to survive without it.

His home was a warehouse, and like any other businessman, he took good care of it. There were many different items, ranging from slot machines to car parts. The dining and sleeping area was effectively made of things he found scavenging. The offices used in the past for business were too revealing, so Philip purposefully kept them dirty. Also, he could never allow himself to be too far or too separated from the goods. That was his way of making up being separated from his family.

Las Vegas was not a small city, and even in its prime, required having a vehicle to go from point A to point B. Fortunately, it was situated in a flat valley, relatively easy to get by without a motorized vehicle, using various types of bicycles. When it came to procuring goods and scavenging, it was always better to come in unnoticed. Philip owned an electric tricycle that had an option to be manually propelled with space for storage in the back. It was powerful and practical but not good looking. He finally decided to walk, putting on his best clothes.

The sun was setting, and it was still scorching hot outside. Philip regretted his decision, but it was too late to change his mind. He was beginning to sweat. Catching every shade he could find on the way; he finally arrived at the Park. Though its name suggested there would be plenty of greenery around, it was filled with shrubs, cacti, and tumbleweed. The pecan stood out in that crowd with its massive trunk and branches and green leaves covering its surface.

"She is not coming," he thought, waiting patiently beneath the pecan. His curious nature led him to examine the tree, go around it in circles. He was nervous. An occasional passer-by would disturb his erratic thoughts, forcing Philip to compose himself.

Fifteen minutes later, he was certain she would not come. Stubborn as he was, Philip wasn't about to give up that easily. He sat on the ground and leaned onto the pecan tree. He saw nothing but rocks and withered plants around him. But the terrain he was sitting on was soft as a pillow. Before looking down, he used his hands to touch the ground and was cut. Razor-sharp green leaves sprouted. They were not there moments ago, though. Patches of grass were few and far between in Old Vegas, but almost none existed in Sunset Park after the lake dried decades ago.

"What the hell is going on here?" He jumped from the ground and saw a circle of grass surrounding the pecan. At first, he thought he imagined things. Then he was sure he did. There was no point in asking anyone else. They would say that patch of grass was always there. In all his deliberation, he forgot to notice everything around him turned dark. "There is no point in waiting any longer. I'll go home." The night was the time for the Raiders, and he knew that well, so he rushed home.

Philip sat at his ancient portable computer, waiting for something to happen. Even though like most of his neighbors, he could access Zetwork at any given moment and lose himself in virtual reality, there was something about it that made him feel connected to the past. The device was probably over two centuries old but made in such a sturdy way that even time couldn't do anything to it. All it needed was an electrical input, and it would light up. It was noisy, and the whirring fans made it all but impossible to focus on anything else. In time, he learned to accept the sound, even love it, and find peace in it.

For the past few months, Philip had a project. He would scan the nearby area, searching for a signal, any signal beyond those purposefully sent out by the Zzone. Usually, he would only catch static. On most days, that was enough for him. Today it wasn't the case. He needed something more, whatever sign to alleviate his pain and soothe his nerves. Even the sound of fans was too much for him.

So Philip put on headphones, a thing he did only once in a blue moon, as they severely limited his ability to hear any sound. In Old Vegas, especially, such a thing was risky. When he turned them on, there was only a familiar crackling and popping sound. Scanning a while with no success, he felt like giving up. Then, he remembered the headphones had a very old switch on them. It was used to scan frequencies people used long before the Great War. The chances of finding something there were equal to zero. Having nothing better to do, he gave it a chance.

He started rotating the small button. Immediately he heard something unfamiliar, a noise that shouldn't be there. It was chaotic, unruly, and wild. But it was in no way static. The noise was alive, and it changed in an instance, going from high to low and vice versa. It was something resembling music, Philip deduced. He tried listening more carefully, and he thought he was able to make up some words.

"My heart should be well-schooled
'Cause I've been fooled in the past
But still, I fall in love so easily
I fall in love too fast."

Those were the exact words he needed to hear; he didn't know how to utter them. Before what he was now certain was music, ended, Philip decided to record it. He was no expert in ancient music, nor was that knowledge was generally available or sought after. He knew who would know more about it and decided to visit him that very instant.

The house conveniently located close to old Interstate 15 was not so hard to reach. It was far away, though, and using a tricycle to get there dangerous. Finding nothing better to do, he jumped at the opportunity, even with all risks involved. Philip's grandfather was old, even by contemporary standards. It was said he lived through the Great War that ended civilization and grew together with the Zzone. Philip called him Gramps for short.

"Your generation will never know the likes of them. Hell, their music was more than a century old when I was born, "the grandfather said after listening to the recording. An array of rhythms played together, distinctive tone colors, and performance techniques topped by improvisation to make the tune off-beat. That's jazz. Goddamn legend Chet Baker. Where did you get this?"

"I've recorded it from an unknown source."

"Wait, you don't even know where this came from?" Gramps was visibly upset. He then smiled, showing he was intrigued at the same time. "Think about it, boy. Where do you think it came from?"

"I am not sure. I changed the frequency of my headphones to the spectrum no one uses these days. And then, I manually changed frequencies. I really don't know." Philip shrugged.

"Of course, you don't. Why would you? Like all knowledge of the ancient world, it is undesirable in the Zzone."

He was again turning angry, and Philip felt it was due to his deep hatred for the government.

"It feels like a gramophone record. But it isn't. Tell me, how did it make you feel? Can you at least describe that?" Gramps asked.

"Sad, I guess." Philip shrugged again. "You know, there is this girl.."

"...Just sad?" Gramps' interrupted as his eyes turned even viler. "These unfiltered emotions, they are lost to time.

And you tell me they make you feel sad? Sad is not a feeling. Being at the counter drunk pouring your heart out to the bartender after getting your heartbroken for the third time is. It gives you the chills, makes you want to kill yourself. But that's what being human is all about. You go through it, and life goes on. This is a song of remembrance. And there you thought you were sad." He smirked.

"But she…" Philip tried to justify his reaction.

"…Listen to the trumpet boy. Only listen to it. Don't talk or think. It touches your soul. And his voice. There are a poignance and sweetness in his voice. Don't you want to sing it along." Gramps took a bottle of very old brandy from the shelf. "Now, bring me two glasses from the counter over there."

"I don't drink."

"I never asked you if you drank or not. You are a man now, and this is what men do."

Balkanizzonation

The Balkans was a troubling region even in the pre-Zzone era, a place where borders did not exist and were present at every step. Though embedded within the European superstate, this area always lacked in economic and political prosperity. The dissolution of nation-states into chaos and anarchy was only stopped there by the sheer will of villagers who refused to wage yet another meaningless conflict for the sake of one country or another. The only thing they had and would always keep was the fruitful land they had tilled and died for since time immemorial.

Times have changed, but the Balkans remained frozen in time as the region was divided by the new powers that be and connected by those same ordinary people who worshipped the ground they walked upon. And they certainly did not want to be left without it. That is why even after a hundred years of success within the United Zzone Federation, it represented a troubling region. Simple divisions into Western and Eastern, Northern or Southern Zzone could never quite grasp the troublesome Balkan folk's complexities and simplicities. There were even rumors about a greater Balkan Zzone, but due to the term's historical connotations and a failed common state project in the past, that idea was abandoned. Therefore, it was one of the few remaining regions in the world which constantly changed the number of Zzones it had. Evil tongues said that the mischievous Balkan folks made fun of the system and exploited it for their benefit.

Like all human creatures, they felt the urge to prove their existence to others and would give everything to satisfy that desire. In many other cultures, such a feeling was exacerbated by the pursuit of more material goods. But in the Balkans, this desire was expressed by a single line, have more than thy neighbor. No matter how poor or rich your neighbor was, as long as you had more than them, no one could come close to you. That is at least what westerners believed, thinking it was only natural for all people south of some imaginary line to behave differently. A border, geographical limit between Central Europe, civilization, and the Balkans, oriental despotism, as one philosopher put it, was right there on the Danube river.

The truth was often more sinister. Small Zzones were frightened of larger ones and hungry for power. Local rulers desired to obtain it by any means necessary. Even though the nation-states they constituted were long gone, these Zzones were too afraid of disappearing in the same manner their predecessors did centuries before, consumed by war and ethnic conflict. So in their struggle to keep the little power they had, they often sacrificed everything they pretended to stand for.

Before the Greatest War, this fear, fueled by outside factors, made the nation-states of the Balkans susceptible to foreign influence. So, when the chance arose to receive nuclear bombs from both sides, they agreed without a doubt. Mindless masses cheered for the powerless leaders, not imagining these weapons would be used against them. No one asked the villagers for their opinion. And like many times in the past, they were wrong. Playing marionettes to the powerful sides, the Balkan folk paid the highest price and lost most of their population.

Beautiful and, at the time, still clean rivers were poisoned by radiation, forests withered and died, the air turned toxic. Thanks to the Košava wind, the effect was not as strong in the central region. Closer to the coasts, winds from the sea secured those regions survived relatively unscathed. But in the coming decades, super-resistant forests that rose from the radioactive ashes once again covered the continent. With no one left to blame, the local rulers turned their sights on nature as the source of all evil. And the continual destruction their predecessors started resumed until the Zzone system was established. The forests fought back as much as they could but to no avail.

It was difficult to blame ordinary people. After spending too much time inside the domes, they entered a world unlike the one they left. A new generation of villagers was born, those unaware of the once rich land they walked on—a land soaked in blood. Younger generations only knew of the stories their parents told them. Finally, outside, eager to do and make something of themselves, they needed a leader and a goal, someone to follow and something to achieve.

It was not long after that the world government was formed. However, United Zzone Federation was interested in the Balkans to connect the different regions and cultures over the three continents. Bridging the gap was not a new thing though it was advertised as such. It was a continuation of the millennia-old policy. And like the policies of the past, it had nothing good in the store for ordinary folk. They appeared to be compliant on the surface, and for the oblivious and careless world government, they were nothing more.

But before this new world government managed to integrate the region into the Zzone system, it had to go through many changes that would eventually shape the

Balkans and the world itself. The focus was to obliterate the national spirit, soul, and culture that existed before the Greatest War. These things brought the conflict in the first place, they argued, and it had no place in the modern world if humanity was to survive. One of the first policies was related to population exchange and making people idolize and accept a new identity given to them, loyalty to the Zzone they lived in. Later it was followed by inexplicable changes in goods produced, all to have those who remembered the time before the war puzzled. The confusion policies lasted until the goal was seemingly reached.

Having lost their identities and gained the Federation's respect, the authorities believed this region's problems stopped. Yet the people of the Balkans rebelled for no apparent reason. One could say they were used to fighting the autocratic governments, that they did not wish to conform to the standards, if history before the Greatest War was to be trusted. For centuries, the Balkans in the West were eponymous with tribalism and the backward, primitive way of thinking. Barbarians, hordes. Not even the Greatest War, which symbolized the ending of the world, managed to change that.

Those same villagers that grew up in the domes found it impossible to survive in such conditions. Even their new identities were no match for the power of nature. They found evidence of their ancestors in the rubble of the cities, on the mountaintops and river valleys, and rediscovered themselves. After that, there was no going back to the old new ways. They waited for the right time to act, to take back the ground they walked upon, the ground their ancestors enriched by giving their lives for it. It was one thing they could never forget. No conditioning could change that.

Having noticed that, the United Zzone Federation implemented a series of new laws. The more restrictive the laws were, the more rebellious the people became. It threatened to undermine the whole new world project as other Zzones joined in the protest. A new dichotomy was about to be created, a new status quo. Initial attempts to crush the rebellion by force caused too many casualties, too many for the world with a diminishing population. This realization and fast-acting made it so that a change from within was needed and welcomed. It was a welcome surprise for the world already used to constant changes.

Furthermore, they took their robotic companions' advice into account and investigated similar cases worldwide only to discover their policies did not work as they expected them to. Human history is as feeble as human hearts, and feeling devotion for something larger than oneself is a universal feeling that needs to be nurtured. It was only a matter of how to make the Zzone that thing instead of backward national identity. An empire built on bloody foundations would end in blood, and United Zzone Federation knew that well.

No one was to be left alienated, and all humans were to create a common identity, it was proclaimed one day. Following Zetwork's human improvement plan, all humans species were to undergo this process, with newly resurrected Neanderthals, Denisovans, and Floresians alongside their fellow Sapiens. Once and for all, the definition of what made one human would expand. What designated someone as human from the planet Earth would no longer be related to the area one was born in, their nationality, skin color, religion, and other factors. Zetwork envisioned one xenophilic human culture.

Only decades later, this utopian dream began to take shape. Time and time again, it proved impossible for everyone to peacefully coexist, no matter how accepting the society was. Denisovans almost completely blended in with Sapiens, while Neanderthals and Floresians were forced to the fringes of society as UZF shifted back to being an autocracy. Zetwork could not allow another cycle of human downfall and fragmentation to occur as its ultimate goal was to help it. After decoding an obscure line from work stored in its archives, it finally had the right answer.

Machines are made to take things literally, and no matter how advanced an AI was, it always first thought of the most logical solution. The line that stated, "The fault, dear Brutus, is not in our stars, But in ourselves, that we are underlings," was interpreted as a call to speed up human exploration of the Solar system. The only way to stop the Balkanization and destiny of the new world was to find a common enemy outside. For the first time in history, all humans joined in on one project to finally locate alien life and destroy it.

Glurbs

1

Throughout much of history, humans have perceived themselves as superior to all other creatures. Myths of their divine origin and their place at the crown of creation are found in religions reaching back thousands of years. Even during scientifically enlightened times, this conviction of supremacy has not been shaken. They considered themselves the masters of the planet Earth, the pinnacle of evolution, and the only rational and moral species in the world of unconscious creatures red in tooth and claw. But not all have agreed with this sentiment. Some viewed humankind in a very different light.

In the world of Glurbs, humans were a delicacy very few could taste and thoroughly enjoy due to their status as galactic harlequins. But after the unnecessary and risky conquest of a few human colonies, it all changed. In recent centuries, humanity spread its arms eager to grasp the universe, unaware of how vast it truly was. However, this did not go as well or as planned by them. They were able to eradicate and conquer the few space-faring species in their vicinity, but that was as far as they could go using rudimental technology. That is why hundred-year missions were sent to far away habitable systems to speed up the expansion. These worlds were considered ripe for the taking, but in the eyes of interstellar empires, the human colonists were the ones easier to pick off.

For most Glurbonians, they were no more than despicable little pests and quite more annoying. However, as times change, so do Glurbs. Soon after conquering those unlucky few, they debated what kind of purpose humans could have in the Empire of Glurbs. Most agreed their destruction was the simplest and most desirable outcome. More imaginative minds speculated that humans should be kept as pets or for entertainment due to their delicate structure and tolerable intelligence. There were even those who desired to try something rather unorthodox for Glurbonians with them. They tried dissecting and preparing meals from them. A few specimens were sent to the most eccentric Glurbonian chefs specializing in this mostly unknown and arcane skill. Their final verdict was that humans were "an acquired taste" but could still be used as nutrients in the lack of other, better resources.

However, under the guidance of its most trusted intelligent machines, the human dominion decided not to react and declare war on the almighty Empire of Glurbs.

They were still hatchlings born into a world where space travel was the most basic and understood technology. For them, this young industry, they thought of as space exploration, was nothing more than a desire to achieve their own fundamental needs as a species. To colonize, make empires, and exploit, do the same things their ancestors did on their home planet, and humanity was still recovering from, that was their goal. But what they failed to realize was that the universe was much more diverse and infinitely larger than the human mind's limited conception could ever imagine. They believed these things could conceivably inspire some future laws to determine their fate in the larger universe they slowly became a part of.

But as galactic luck would have it, their desire came true in a very different manner. After the first unsuccessful attempts to bring human flesh to the market and present it as an exotic specialty failed, Glurbonian chefs seemingly shelved the idea for a better time. However, some side effects of consuming flesh rich in so many protein types appealed to the more liberal circles in Glurbonian capital. Cured human flesh was distributed illegally as a sort of medicine with narcotic properties. Its curative and addictive properties made it increasingly popular among the ever-widening circle of Glurbonians. With the continual supply of fresh humans from the colonies, the illegal business bloomed.

It was only a matter of time before other alien species developed a taste for them. The galactic market, like any other, functioned based on supply and demand. Under pressure from many notable individuals, the ruling body decided to legalize the production, distribution, and use of various meat products of human origin. However, this move did not go without opposition. Some parties claimed that eating human flesh was unhealthy, and its addictive properties could have an unknown effect on the Glurbonian psyche in the long run. But these protesters were either outvoiced or bought out by those who earned excessive amounts of money by trading the said products.

Glurb Prime rapidly began cultivating these vile creatures on one of its less developed moons. At first, due to a lack of experts in the field, it wasn't easy to keep the samples alive and healthy long enough to make them profitable. But as fortunes came in succession, more funds were transferred and awarded to laboratories investigating humans. No one thought of asking humans themselves about their physiology. After an accidental breakthrough that brought its finder a Glurb Award, the most prestigious award in that part of the galaxy, industrial human production was at least a feasible undertaking. Billions upon billions of humans were grown in captivity; their life spans accelerated to make them reach full maturity sooner.

Human sausages became increasingly popular out of all available products due to their unique flavor originating from the microflora in the human gut. But no part of humans was ever thrown away as their production was still pretty expensive. Their brittle bones were crushed and powdered, making them an ideal spice. Glurbonian chefs only failed to find the purpose of the muscular protrusions on top of their bodies that seemed to control the remaining portions called brains. "Such a waste," said one of the butchers while throwing the entire human nervous system out in the trash.

Brands advertising for fresh human meat often featured humans giving two thumbs up, though it was doubtful these "humans" approved how their species was treated at such places. Dried and cured products were devoid of such representations, instead only showing cut pieces of the final product being consumed with expensive liquor. Nevertheless, humans became widely known throughout the galaxy thanks to these and other similar commercial services. "Look at how happy and smiling they are," Glurbonian housewives said on her way to the market. If only they knew humans could communicate in a similar way

Glurbonians did, perhaps they would train a few of them to do advertising.

At the same time, this overproduction of humans made the moon practically inhabitable. Furthermore, the waste products that covered most of the habitable zone were threatening to pour out into space and reach Glurb Prime itself. This was possible due to the thin atmosphere and low gravity of the moon itself. Even so, it took time until some Glurbonians finally noticed the issue and reacted to it. "Those humans cause pollution with their gasses and waste products that we cannot use in any way," was their main argument. More aggravating circumstances for humans followed as it was decided their diet was to be modified according to the findings presented and the ruling body's decisions. This caused them to become sickly and reduced income from the sales, yet no one dared contradict the law. It was one of the few things Glurbonians were unable to do. And they took great pride in it.

As it usually happens on most planets of this universe, a group contradicting and counteracting the one, as mentioned earlier, sprung into existence. It quickly gathered followers, some being there from purely benevolent and xenophilic intents, eager to help genuinely, and the others who joined to spite their rivals and enemies. There were, of course, those able to smell the profit all the attention brought.

However, as the membership increased, so did the various opinions and beliefs, causing the group to fracture into many smaller ones. Some groups advocated for the so-called human rights; others only wanted humans to get better living conditions, seeing how their exploding population caused them to be bred in ever-smaller spaces. There were even those who dared equal humans and Glurbonians. But these people were in the minority, and no one took them seriously. Most Glurbonians were moderate and always strived to find balance in any issue at hand. "Why eat some but pet the others?" was one of their most popular slogans, related to the fact some humans were considered smarter and more appealing based on the color of their skin. "Such a silly notion," one friend told to the other, "I find them all equally distasteful."

2

For years and years, the Empire of Glurbs prospered with its exclusive commodity dominating the market. Trillions of humans continued to be abused in many ways on Glurbonian farms while their numbers in the far reaches of the universe barely crossed a dozen billion. But in the shadows, something sinister was creeping, the thing no one ever expected to affect Glurbonians in any way. Due to a diet rich in human flesh replacing traditional and historically dominant ones, which mainly consisted of fruits, vegetables, and marine animals, a once peaceful space-faring race turned into a power-hungry machine whose only desire was more of everything. And it seemed to every Glurbonian that it was their destiny, purpose of living to extend the reaches of the Empire as furthest as possible. The number of pacifists in their ranks slowly decreased as they were the ones who rejected to consume human flesh, which introduced hormonal changes. And those changes had adverse effects on those who did. Starting with increased aggression and ending with more children. "For posterity," Glurbonians yelled, waving their war flags. They forgot the fact there were times in the past when progeny was safer when there were no wars. This infinite greed, insatiable hunger threatened to swallow the galaxy.

But Glurbonians were not alone in their gluttony. Many other prosperous civilizations around the galaxy were going through what can only be described as a "reawakening" process. Genes that have for eons been considered redundant and useless were reactivated thanks to the human diet. And these other civilizations were hungry for power, for more territory, and more humans. Occasional skirmishes over a few bordering star systems more often and more quickly turned to wars. At the same time, the armament race started and caused the empires to stockpile weaponry. A galactic war was something unimaginable, indescribable, and wholesomely incomprehensible. In all of the galaxy's known history, it only happened once before, but its records were lost to time. This one threatened to undo eons of development and bring back the galaxy to the dark ages before the emergence of sentient beings. Perhaps it was better that way.

The conflict was temporarily stopped by the sheer might of the Glurbonian fleet that decimated many of their enemies' spaceports. In a sudden counterattack, a coalition of alien species managed to reach Glurb Prime and steal a million living, breathing humans from its moon. Many more died by being exposed to the vacuum of space. This theft crippled the Glurbonian economy, which was already very susceptible to changes. For years its became more dependent on the export of only a limited type of commodities originating from one source and when that source was threatened, so was the economy. It gave the competitors an edge against the Empire of Glurbs. For a while, all sides thought they were winning, as is the case in wars spanning limitless light-years. But in fact, this conflict turned into a war of attrition, as each side awaited the other to make a move. In the meantime, humans were unwillingly and unwittingly disseminated across the galaxy, thus becoming the most widespread species in the galaxy.

This issue did not seem like a large or very important one at the time. But with so many specimens on so many different planets with as many alien species each liking a suitable blend of humans, the chances were something was going to go bad. Not minding the occasional death here and there, Glurbonian enemies failed to notice the epidemic. They were too busy fighting the war of attrition, and by the time they realized, it was too late. Three whole systems were lost to the terrible affliction believed to have been caused by an enzyme secreted by the human liver. Realizing this menace could also affect them greatly, Glurbonians called for a truce. The fight to contain this outbreak required all sides to work together, which for the first time in many eons, most empires agreed to do.

Like the rest of the galaxy, the human-animal as the species came to be known, was for its own and the security of the galaxy, locked away to spend days in peaceful slumber in its part of the galaxy. To secure not one of the competing empires would profit from them more than necessary, a transparent and impenetrable shield was placed around their neighboring systems, replacing the exclusion zone that once prevented entrance. Its purpose was to create the illusion that space, as humans knew it was indeed theirs to see, but it always remained to prove it is unreachable. Of course, it was not the humans' fault for their biology and what it did to other alien species. But someone had to take the blame before the galaxy.

For this reason, the remaining humans were hated, despised, and persecuted. But due to many other reasons, they remained a necessary evil. The galaxy needed food, and these creatures were uniquely adaptable to different nutrients. Intergalactic currencies lost value so fast that they ceased to exist. The only and most powerful currency that remained was humans. That is how humans became the most widely spread race in the cosmos, but not in the way they may have dreamed. Many centuries later, they would take their chance to be much more.

An excerpt from the Emperor's private notes:

"We tend to neglect the fact we evolved from animals as well. Our distant ancestors were feeding on other animals. This so-called human diet effect is nothing more but us reverting to our roots. As I look at my fellow Glurbonians, I try to understand what it is exactly that made them act so differently than before. What is undoubtedly true is that our understanding of the cosmos and attitude towards it undoubtedly changed. Moreover, interpersonal communication is now necessarily followed by a wide arrange of facial expressions, most of which I never thought were possible for a Glurbonian. The chemicals in our human diet intensify much of it, which leads to discord within the population.

Everyone is more observant and more susceptible to others. Earlier, while I was still a young ruler, people only either bowed or lowered their heads out of respect. My family and friends never had what the word for it; a serious expression about them is. There was no reason to; it didn't exist. These latest changes bring, perhaps only unconsciously, a certain uneasiness and elevated hormone levels. This phenomenon could be what humans referred to as stress. The war forever changed the Empire of Glurbs, but I sense we were changed more by these creatures we eat. But I cannot blame my compatriots when even I find their flesh irresistible.

I fear for the future. Even though the peace we arranged is set to last a thousand generations, I wonder what kind of world I am leaving for my successors. In essence, we have become slaves to our diet to humans who are themselves our slaves. How cruel can fate be? If only I hadn't ordered the attack on their colonies back then, no one would have died. Still, I was young and eager to prove myself in action. Then perhaps I have deserved this slow and never-ending punishment."

3

Humans have completely blended in with their masters within a galactic century, often acquiring their characteristics necessary for survival. They evolved into hundreds, maybe even a thousand different species when those outside the dominion of the Empire of Glurbs are taken into account. However, the nature of the human-animal remained unchanged. Once again, no one thought of looking deep beneath the human psyche, beneath the vanity and the masks they displayed. They were the only living creatures severed from their instincts, hence the sickest species ever coming into existence in all the galaxy. Aliens never thought of reading about and listening to what humans had to say about themselves. And if they did, they would find out that as one man whose name was lost centuries ago said, humans were, "relatively speaking, the most mangled of all the animals, the sickliest, the one most dangerously strayed from its instincts."

And no matter how integrated, how uplifted human-animals were perceived to be in some parts of the galaxy, to most, they remained half-animals well adapted to war, prowling, and adventure. For these reasons, humans proved to be the most resourceful and fearsome warriors. From being considered food, they attained companions' status and were even given special permits to be used as fodder in smaller skirmishes. There was one place these creatures could exhibit their natural talents and tendencies for violence. The Galactic Arena, created after the end of the galactic war, served as a place for those less fortunate to compete and earn freedom. Simultaneously, it was a place where illicit activities took place.

Within these confines of society and peace, no longer ruled by survival instincts alone, the evolved human-animals faced another existential threat. Their animal instincts did not disappear in being suppressed and forced underground, rather turning against them, forcing them to punish themselves. There was no place more suitable for that than the Arena. And punish and slaughter each other they did, year after year, season after season so fiercely that the other alien species of lower rank refused to compete. For them, a quick death was preferable to fighting the demented human-animals.

A strange occurrence was noticed after a dozen cycles, the fact that those who were closer to the original human-animal were more successful. These selection and mutation processes degenerated the species in so many ways. Like domesticated animals, their brothers and sisters who have generations ago stopped being human were frail and weak. They required extra care, special nutrients, and a lot of love. Yet love was one thing they could never get. Unbeknownst to them, they exemplified what forced evolution could do a species. Psychological evaluation of one such creature showed what kind of animals they have become. When forced to relieve the toughest moments, the specimen exhibited a sense of unrestrained pride but no fear.

"Tsk tsk," he said, looking at the other competitors. "What passes for a human these days, tsk. It feels like anything barely resembling us is taken to compete. It is no wonder the Arena's popularity decreases after each cycle. Just look at those poor excuses. I'll bet they haven't even seen a pureblood like me in their lives. I can trace back roots to the first colonists accepted into the Empire of Glurbs. What is it they have to show for, other than a head with two arms and two legs? I win because I am the strongest, the smartest, the most perfect among them." When fighting and killing, this human felt only exhilaration, the rush. There was no other emotion, only desire to kill. Supported and further encouraged by the loud cheers from the Arena crowd, he felt like an ancient gladiator, slicing his competitors one at a time.

The applause came, the final one coming after all the slaves were defeated. The man stood alone and empty before the pool of blood and bones of his defeated enemies. He looked up and, for a moment, felt immensely larger and stronger than the aliens in the crowd. No longer in the Arena, he was as high as the sky and even more distant and unreachable. His overwhelming popularity only grew larger each cycle. The Master of Ceremonies announced him as the undisputed champion of this competition. "Yes, I am the irrefutable champion," he thought. There was no need for him to say anything; the crowd already knew his face well. "I am the best!"

Having spent so much time with and among human-animals, Glurbonians never before thought of entering the mind of one of them, never desired to get to know them better. Humans were and remained just food and pets for them. When the Emperor's high commander saw and experienced what was in this human's mind, he began to shiver and sweat. Fear mixed with similar emotions he never encountered even while fighting in the galactic war against alien forces so uncanny came over him. He shook and collapsed to the floor. "Terminate him," was his final order. "And then all the others."

HMS

Excerpt from the galactic bestseller: On humans and other vexatious species by Thal'gru from Scriv'ox Research Cooperative

The galaxy is teeming with life, and that is clear to any moderately developed civilization. Those who have no notion of the universe outside their solar system fail to understand this simple truth and instead believe they are alone. Uplifting such species is universally frowned upon as the delicate balance between great powers would be shattered in doing so. What is not forbidden is to monitor those brutes, and with the galaxy being what it is, everyone wanted information.

For millennia the debate was led as to what to do with one particularly pesky civilization, blessed with ideal conditions for life, so ideal that some argued if it was even possible for such a civilization to exist in the first place without the interference of some higher power. Yet despite all efforts, no proof was found it did. When a consensus was reached to monitor their progress, the galaxy greeted it with exuberant joy. There was something unique about Earth's inhabitants; their actions were often irrational and unpredictable, their thoughts so logical and reasoned. Until the next moment when the roles switched.

Many of the brightest minds in the galaxy debated on the causes of such behavior, some rising to stellar fame in the process. In time, this kind of surveillance grew into a game of chance, and the minds observing the behavior of "HMS" species started guessing what kind of actions some individuals would take. However, any interference was strictly punished as the planet's location was kept secret from the public. Despite the obvious desire of authorities to stop it, the interest in this species continued to grow. It was only a matter of time before ordinary galactic citizens felt they deserved the right to do so as well. A committee was formed and decided to allow anyone willing to understand such an erratic and illogical species better. It was the first of many committees to be formed regarding this species.

Centuries later, which in galactic terms is a blink of an eye, the situation changed. Though the society on Earth evolved beyond expectations following a global conflict, it was still not advanced enough to meet the minimum criteria for joining the galactic union. That did not mean the interest in the species subsided. On the contrary, every one of these HMS beings had their fan club. Some considered them jesters, clowns who entertained the masses; others thought of them as nothing more than a fad. Observing them became the favorite pastime for many galactic species and led to many interesting phenomena, unobserved before.

HMS's mind is a peculiar thing in a galaxy that explored almost everything. It can withstand extensive hardships, compute immense possibilities, yet one small change can reduce it to a mushy collection of neurons. Their mind is their strongest tool, which at the same time makes them the weakest of all intelligent species. As its primary goal is survival, it evolved to search for patterns and meaning. So, when all the possible meanings were found, their brains continued searching and found meaning where there was none. Though varying and diverse, conspiracy theories all had one purpose: to appease the brain and make it feel like it was in control. They were afraid of being watched, being under someone or something else's control, so they retreated to themselves. It was true. Someone was watching but from hundreds of light-years away.

"The situation escalated quickly," argued one of the most arduous proponents of leaving the species behind to fend off for itself.

"We need more content," was the opinion of others.

Still, most observers loved the fact no one could do anything to influence these creatures' lives and found joy in following their everyday activities. It was all a matter of chance, day by day. A single HMS creature could average over a billion followers, predicting or guessing its every move. Conflicts on Earth, smaller or greater in scale, sent shockwaves to the galaxy. Most of the time, these conflicts were beneficial as they prevented similar things from happening elsewhere in the galactic union. The galaxy knew HMS creatures better than they knew themselves. But it kept aside until the time was right to greet them.

HMS exclusion zone spanned a dozen light-years from Sol, their star. Trade, transportation, and any activities were prohibited in that region, which wasn't much of a burden for the union. Sol system was located on the fringes of one arm of the galaxy, a place so devoid of any activity or resources that only those brave or foolish enough desired to visit it.

Yet, it didn't stop a loyal community of followers from making small habitats in the region. These outposts mostly functioned as tourist attractions and sold various goods supposedly taken from the Sol system. Among the most popular items, pieces of Earth's moon were sought for as interesting relics. It was one of the unique phenomena in that part of the galaxy as most habitable planets had at least two moons orbiting them. No one could or desired to examine their authenticity. Most wanted items included 6-D printed copies of popular personal items. With so many humans to choose from, these items were produced on the spot, trinkets of low value to bring back home as souvenirs.

Besides gift shops, the outposts included resting area, refueling stations, and mandatory health check-up booths. These booths were standard for millennia, and besides treating physical and mental ailments, they tested for the presence of parasites, contaminants, and unknown materials. One of the outposts became notorious for its pursuit of knowledge regarding HMS species. As no direct contact was ever established or allowed, visitors were greeted by and presented various theories based on limited data.

"Such delicate species. Did you know they require unique conditions to survive?" Ne'eri, one of the Glurbonian observers, asked his friend.

"I am afraid I did not," Metrivurtu replied. He was a member of the Croquis- Ierlin Martial Alliance."I never took them for such an extraordinary species. I assumed they needed…"

"And don't get me started on their mating rituals," Ne'eri interrupted. "So complex, so irrational. I wonder how these things came into being in the first place."

Metrivurtu was at a loss for words. It was not uncommon for his friend to interrupt him midsentence, but this was already a third time today. He waited for Ne'eri to finish his soliloquy about fascinating HMS species. It was a story he repeated over and over again. The first couple of times, Metrivurtu found it interesting to hear, to learn more about the species, but then, as an asteroid stuck on a loop, the story became familiar and dull.

"And then their bodily functions shut down. It is a process they are aware of but don't try to fight. Crazy, huh?"

"Fascinating!" Metrivurtu exclaimed. He knew that pretending to do so would not hurt his friend's feelings. "Let's order two more Glurbonian ales." He signaled the waiter to bring more drinks. Then he decided to tell a story as well. "What if I told you they are watching us right now, those HMS creatures. How about it, Ne'eri?"

"That's doubtable. We would have known about it." Though he seemed calm, Ne'eri was intrigued by the idea and started looking around for invisible listening devices.

Metrivurtu smiled. "It is true, you know. They have these things called telescopes that peer deep into the galaxy, further than we know."

"Impossible! Their scanners are not nearly advanced enough to see planets and moons, let alone outposts like this one." Ne'eri became increasingly interested in the story and tried to find logic in it. He was easily fascinated by anything related to HMS creatures, especially things he didn't know about.

"That's what they want you to believe. How can you know they don't have the technology to do so? They are fooling everyone, don't you see? It is just a matter of time before they decide to take over the galaxy. The union should react and do something about them soon." He was certain he had Ne'eri fooled with that final touch.

"I still can't believe it."

Metrivurtu knew he had to give him more, something Ne'eri could use to make a new theory and retell it for years. "Why do you think the union made the exclusion zone this big? They are afraid of them, that's why." Seeing no change in Ne'eri's expression, he decided to use the oldest trick in existence. "Think for yourself. If you don't believe me, test it out. You'll see. Trust me."

They gulped down the ales in a second.

"I am sure now. You wouldn't lie to me; you know how much I care about this. Would you?" He believed in his friend's story. Ne'eri rushed away to his interstellar port to search for more information.

Having convinced him to investigate, Metrivurtu returned to his habit of collecting unique pieces of HMS culture. Their lives, though he would never admit it, gave meaning to his.

Interview with the
Vampiress

Isidor was happy as his show recently gained popularity among the middle-class citizens, his target audience. Every week he would bring in a new guest, a new stranger from the fringes of the Zzone, and talk with them about other races, conspiracy theories, the dangers of the Oblivion, and anything else popular that week on Zetwork. This week's guest has, unsurprisingly, incited the communication by offering something almost forgotten to the mix.

"We are ready to start," a robotic voice uttered. Speedy, his loyal companion, was top of the line AI. Even at this time, when AI surpassed human intellect and capabilities, they were considered no more than companions and given names as such.

"Bring me in," Isidor replied, thus starting the uploading process to the Zetwork. Isidor and his guest would naturally remain present in their bodies, discussing live from his studio in La Jolla Farms. He never liked crowds and rather enjoyed the company of his AI, so there were never any other people around. As for security, he felt confident Speedy could and would do everything to protect him.

"Virtual reality recording started. Safety warning: Objects in the mirror are not real."

"Yeah, yeah, yeah, I know that already," Isidor dismissed. His view was suddenly overlayed by another image coming from the Zetwork. In such a way, he was able to be in the real and constructed world simultaneously. People's avatars and characters began appearing in front of his eyes. "Hello, guys, and welcome to yet another episode of Zcast, a series that explores unique denizens of our lovely Zzone. My name is Isidor Z, and I will be your host. Please remain calm while establishing a connection to Zetwork."

"Note: San Diego Zzone authorities publicly support this broadcast," Speedy interrupted.

"We have a special guest today. Many believe vampires are just tales and myths used to scare children and feeble-minded in the times before the collapse that was the Greatest War. Those who survived lived to tell the tale, or did they?" At that moment, the counter on his wrist signaled enough members have joined to start the session. "Ladies and gentlemen, she was said to have a unique physical appearance, and she is right behind this door." Virtual doors in Isidor's channel appeared and opened. "Everyone welcome the Vampiress." He clapped once.

The crowd started to clap virtually as a woman appeared behind the door and entered the lavish and exclusive space of Zcast. She wore a vibrant red robe and possessed long, tapering nails with flowing black hair that concealed her white skin. In Zcast, one could select whatever attire they desired, but the Vampiress only asked for the ability to hover over the ground. In reality, she was entering a closed room but did not seem to mind it.

"You might need this," Isidor said as he handed her the goggles. "Most of our guests like to make direct contact with the audience. It helps them feel relaxed."

"I think I am fine. " Ignoring the whole speech, she took a seat. " Let's skip the shenanigans. I wouldn't say I like this studio. There seem to be no walls here. The holo wall shows nature and outdoors, yet we are here inside trapped like mice."

"I can change it if you don't like it with one word. Just tell me what you would like to see."

"It's your choice; you are the host."

Isidor's peace of mind was stirred. He was confused, rattled by her daring approach. "Please take a seat." Seeing she already did, he sat as well and continued with his already rehearsed speech. "The first question I always ask my guests is, what is your name, and why did you come here."

"Name's June. And for the reasons why I came here, you'll have to wait and see." June, like any other vampire, did not wish to disclose much about her at first. The online audience and the host could not notice that she was slightly nervous upon entering as they were too focused on the constructed image of her. Her nature and experience taught her to avoid enclosed spaces. Yet she knew that even though Isidor felt confident about his adobe, he too was much at risk as her.

"What a spectacularly ordinary name," he thought. "There is no way she is the real thing." Though for a few brief seconds, he felt intimidated by her, Isidor was becoming confident again. "Let me get this off my chest first. I would have expected a vampire's name to sound more like French aristocracy or even Eastern European. For those of you unfamiliar with these arcane terms, " he turned to the holowall, "before the Zzone system was created, Homo Sapiens lived in nation-states and waged wars to preserve them."

"So you do know something about the Old World," June noted. "That is going to make this conversation much easier."

"Well, of course, I do. As my followers already know, my great-grandfather sailed across the ocean from the west." He waved at the empty room. "Now that we got that out of the way, tell me, would you like something to drink?"

"I could use a cup of fresh blood. AB-negative is preferable. If you have O-positive, I'll take it. Make sure you add some ice, though; it spoils fast."

Everyone in the audience smiled. Even the holowall changed to resemble a grinning face.

"Nice one," Isidor smiled forcibly. He could not help but follow his cue, and this was the time for it.

"It's not a joke. I need it to sustain myself but not at this moment." The ice-cold expression on her face signified she wasn't joking.

"I'll be sure to get some next time," he smiled again in the same manner. "Is there anything else I can offer you?"

"Your neck, perhaps? If not, a cup of joe would be fine."

Isidor was taken away by her honesty. He was falling prey to her wily charms. "Black?"

"Darkest one you've got. But no sugar, it's bad for my canines."

A few moments later, Speedy brought two cups of coffee. June took a sip and sat quietly, waiting for Isidor. He took out a notebook and a silver fountain pen, ready to write what she is saying.

"So let me being by asking…"

"Why do you have that? I thought we went live on Zetwork." June interrupted.

"We are. I just like to take notes while talking." He pointed the pen towards her. "See, it is not even real silver. But that gets me wondering, is anything we know about vampires true? Of course, if you are not pretending to be one for fame."

"What pride. You must truly be satisfied with yourself, having a couple of hundred people follow what you have to say." She was hurt on a personal level and retaliated the same. "You still do not believe me, do you? That is one of the reasons I came here today. No, touching silver won't hurt me. I've come here during the day, and I take garlic as an antibiotic. Does that answer your question?"

"That, I must admit, is disappointing."

The audience agreed, and the smiles on their avatars turned to a neutral expression.

Unable to see that, June ignored his comment. "It is strange, though. People forgot about their nations, origin, and customs, yet we all remember tales of supernatural creatures."

"We are all equal in the Zzone, so we don't need to talk about things like that." He was nervous again; it seemed as though she wanted to ruin him.

"Of course, you don't." She smiled. It was a fake smile, and everyone noticed it. "I also don't feel like it for the time being," June stopped to look at his expression. He was sweating. "Thank you, our Overlords, for guiding us through the dark times and into this blissful reality."

Isidor smiled and gulped his drink, visibly shaken.

June blushed. She was visibly excited to see him like that.

"Let's start with some basic information first. Can you tell me how old you are?"

"I think we know each other well enough now so I can say it. Thirty lunar years."

Realizing she was once again toying with him, he asked: "How old are you?"

"Just over two hundred and seventy. I hope you don't have a problem with that."

"Well, you certainly look younger than that. Do you guys agree?" he pointed to the empty room again. Simulated smiles and laughter came from all sides and filled the room. Looking back at her, he added: "You must have been born somewhere around the time of the collapse then. Do you remember it?"

"I was actually all grown up when the world ended. Yet whatever I said about it, people had a hard time accepting it as fact. Many young men, people your age, died for nothing. But that is no different than any other war ever fought."

Fearing she was about to criticize Zzone again, he interrupted. "Then how about now? How do you think life is different today? In what ways is it better?"

This was the first time she noticed him taking the initiative, and that aroused her even further. June kept her composure but was burning inside. Her eyes gave her away. She looked straight at him, gazing into his eyes covered with translucent mirrors. "These modern technologies don't seem to help us much. I don't know if it is something in my vampiric or human nature in general, but I can't get used to having to be available 24 hours a day, so people don't suspect. And that's a little hard, isn't it, considering I'm a vampire. It used to be a lot easier before."

"Well, you can always move to the Oblivion then? That would help you disappear easily." He believed to have made a good, clean joke and his face gleamed with pride.

"You would be surprised," June calmly replied, unaffected by his provocation.

Isidor decided to change topics, having exhausted his questions. "Do you believe in gods?"

"Isn't it superfluous to ask a vampire that question? But yes, despite everything I've been through, in a way, I believe in God."

"Only one?" Isidor felt the tables turning and free enough to be pushy.

"I have to get him back to his place," she thought. "One is quite enough for me. I've lived too long even to think there are so many as the Zzone proclaims."

That answer froze him. The daring game proved to be a challenge for him, and as much as he wanted to end the interview then and there, he was too excited to stop. At the same time, he was frozen stiff from fear.

"You are silent. Could it be you are afraid of me? Afraid of what I have to say is true? How intriguing." June looked at him again and, noticing the sweat pouring down his face, smiled. It was a genuine smile, the first one that day. "Why are you so tense?"

"It's nothing," he calmly replied. There was a dash of fear in his voice. "It's just exhaustion."

That is what she was waiting for, a point she was trying to bring him to. Tender meat is only for the lazy. She knew if she got him excited just a little bit more, he would break. "I feel that today people have nothing to report on. I don't think they ever did, that all this is just one big farce."

"Why do you think people should believe the word you say?" Isidor wanted to stop the interview that instant. But he was unable to utter a single word to Speedy. His throat was dry, palms sweaty. He sat frozen, enchanted by the Vampiress.

"I think you need a massage." June stood up, approached Isidor from behind, and bent over his head. "You are afraid, but don't worry; I will be gentle." The fact he was unable and unwilling to move delighted her. "It is a common misconception that vampires have big fangs. They would only get in the way. Well, look at me, do I look like a vampire to you? After all, do you think I wouldn't have killed you by now if I wanted to do so?"

He wanted to tell her to back off with all his mind, but his body wouldn't listen. Isidor was too weak to order Speedy to stop her. One part of him was excited by what this whole situation could bring. That was one of the reasons he started Zcast in the first place.

"You are the representative of their "bread and circuses" policy. But you can be much more than a slave to them. I can help you with that. Let's see what happens when the cameras stop rolling," June said determinedly. The lights went out in the studio, and Isidor's stream Zcast stopped.

Sometime later, he woke up from his slumber. He noticed two glasses filled with red liquid in front of him. June was sitting opposite of him. "What's going on? Is this my blood?"

"Oh, don't be so melodramatic; it's wine. Cabernet Sauvignon from Napa Valley."

He clasped the glass in one hand, still unsure of what it is and looked at it. Then he brought it closer to his nose and sniffed. "Really? It doesn't smell like Sauvignon. But it has the consistency of wine."

"You've become a real vampire, congrats! Your sight and smell have already sharpened. And yes, it is not Sauvignon. What it is, is a test of your senses. And you have passed." She seemed erratic, excited even.

Isidor noticed her cheeks became redder and immediately touched his neck. There was no scar. "I don't feel so good. I don't feel at all except the rancid taste of that wine."

"That's good. It means you are adapting. Contrary to popular belief, wine is the best substitute for fresh blood." June took a sip of the wine and seemed to enjoy it.

"So, I guess I am a vampire now?" For a moment, he thought of summoning Speedy but gave up on the idea. It would only prevent him from getting to the bottom of this whole situation.

"Technically, vampires don't exist. What I am, what you are now is a result of genetic manipulation using CRISPR technology from the past. It will take some time for your body to adapt fully. But who could explain it to those people?" she pointed to the empty walls around. "Anyway, let's toast."

"Why me?" he asked and realized it no longer mattered."To immortality."

"To immortality indeed." June took another sip.

Isidor slowly raised from his chair, approached her without fear, and looked directly into her eyes. "Cheers," the glasses clacked. They stared at each other and smiled while he returned to his seat. "What happens now?" he asked after a few moments of utter silence.

"What do you mean?" June was stunned by the question. She believed he already understood.

"I mean, what am I supposed to do now that I am a vampire?" He began to think of several ideas.

"Do whatever it is you want. You have the whole eternity to decide that." She spread her hands in a victorious gesture.

Isidor thought for a moment and said: "I don't think I can keep my position any longer. But I also never quite liked it as well." Both of them were still inside the studio, yet it no longer felt like home for him. Speedy was just another machine following the orders it was given, like him until moments ago.

"If you think so, fine. Being a vampire is a curse precisely because you can do anything and feel like doing nothing. You can kill yourself, but that nullifies the purpose of being a vampire. To be alive and not to live, to be always hungry for life, thirsty for all pleasures, and not to be able to achieve them. To dream of life and to live someone's dream. Being a vampire is hell and haven at the same time."

"I didn't know about that."

"You were not supposed to. There is an extra appeal to being a vampire, at least. Other humans find you irresistible in all senses. You could have any female or male you wanted, or you can choose to have only one. Humans may not have evolved to be monogamous; they have evolved to be adaptable. And that is what vampires are, just another adaptation."

"Intruder alert! Intruder alert!" Speedy sounded as his system was back online. "Lockdown in effect. Zzone authorities contacted, approximate arrival in 3 minutes and 33 seconds."

"Time to make a decision. Are you coming or staying inside this cage?" June declared as the lights around them flickered and the walls revealed their true colors.

New York, New York, Old Vegas

1

"Just follow me," Sara stated.

Just behind the wall separating Old Vegas from the rest of New Vegas Zzone lay one of the still-standing monuments to human ingenuity before the Greatest War. Towering buildings that made up what remained of the city were scattered like toys inside the box. The only ones still radiating the idea of order were those glued together in New York-New York. But those also looked like boxes to Philip.

"Come on, hurry up. You know I don't like to be kept waiting." She was persistent.

"In a moment," Philip replied. He was struggling with a shining piece of metal stuck under the broken-down escalator he thought would be worth something on the market. "I almost got it." To his disappointment, what he thought was a valuable material turned out to be an aluminum cigarette coil. It was probably there since time immemorial.

Sara was becoming increasingly impatient with him. She looked at the building in front of them and imagined what was inside of it. Then her eyes moved left to the wall. At that point, it stretched down the I-15. She looked to the south and saw Excalibur and Luxor behind it. For reasons unknown to her, the wall deviated towards Mandalay Bay road, effectively cutting it from Old Vegas, and continued east. She lost interest in looking at it any longer. "What, are you afraid of something?"

Philip came closer to her. "You know why I don't like coming here. It is just creepy. I mean, look at it," he pointed to the rollercoaster.

Sarah was confused and shrugged her shoulders.

"Wait for it," he said after a minute had passed, and nothing happened. Then, an empty train set appeared. It was moving fast towards the first drop. The rattling of chains pulling the set up and the release down was loud enough, but when joined with the prerecorded voices of people screaming in excitement, it created a cacophony of sounds resonating that part of the Strip. Philip felt goosebumps.

"You mean, Manhattan Express?" she asked. "Don't tell me that thing scares you?"

"I am surprised you don't find it scary at all. I don't think I've ever seen you afraid or impressed by something." He was still looking at the Manhattan Express as it made its way across Tropicana Avenue and turned north. Philip was in awe of it and failed to realize his words provoked her.

"You are going on a loop, same way it did just now," Sara sharply replied. "You say all these things over and over again." She hated it when he paid attention to something other than her for longer than a minute. Sara was used to being the queen of Philip's world, and he used every chance to make it appear so.

But there was just something ethereal about the ride that didn't let him be at peace. "Human beings are creatures of habit, of patterns. These patterns we create as children or adults are hard to break, although it is really necessary to do that sometimes."

"What are you even talking about?" She was more confused than irritated at that point.

"As a child, my parents told me I would end up on this ride if I did something wrong. I had nightmares about being stuck up there, all alone like a scarecrow. And I would ride the Manhattan Express over and over again until I was an adult, then a grown man and finally just a skeleton. The only thing that remained of me was the voice that, together with the voices of other disobedient children, circled this hellish ride for eternity. Ever since then, I was unable to ride any roller coaster, though very few except this one remained functional." He paused a second, shifting his gaze from the roller coaster. "That woman is still looking strangely at me. Her right hand is raised, but something is missing. I wonder what it is she wants?"

Sara did not expect to hear such a heartwarming story, and her anger subsided. "That, silly, is the Statue of Liberty, or at least it was until the Greatest War. New Vegans tried to take it and damaged it in the process. They only managed to take the torch, which is now missing."

"I know about the torch. The flame is the symbol of our ancestor's liberty. But what is it the Lady Liberty is showing us? Does she want to say we will never have liberty again as long as the Zzone rules, or is it that the Zzone is the light?"

He was increasingly deviating from the topic, and Sara no longer felt inclined to follow suit. "Let's just try to find a way in, shall we?"

2

It took them a long time to find a way in as all entrances were blocked centuries ago. Old Vegas people generally avoided going into New York-New York ruins due to its haunted roller coaster and proximity to the wall. In the place of the main entrance stood vehicles from the past, as if frozen in time—military equipment from conflicts as old as the Greatest War and scavenged equipment from the newer ones. There was even a broken drone with double Z markings lying in the midst to show the Zzone had nothing to look for in Old Vegas. On their way out of town, New Vegans have also taken memories of Las Vegas with them, including two out of three flashing neon signs decorating the New York-New York entrance.

"I am glad we got to keep at least one of those neon signs," Sara said as she surveyed the area for a possible entry point. Windows on the hotel were broken or barricaded long ago, and to her, the only viable solution was to climb one of the poles that supported Manhattan Express and try to find a way in from above.

"It's a shame we have to keep it underground and under surveillance," Philip replied. "But you know that it isn't only the signs that they stole. They took everything from within as well and left it, like all Vegas, an empty shell."

"Hey, we still have the spirit!" she raised her voice in defiance. "They can never take that from us. No power can."

"You are right. We have each other, and they are alone." He was looking at the empty train above, making another one of its rides with no riders, not at Sara.

She was unsure of whether he meant it seriously or was making one of his usual sarcastic comments. For a few moments, she waited expectantly to see what he would tell her.

He watched the Manhattan Express go up and down, make a loop, disappear inside the building, and then turned to her. "For all it's worth, I am glad I have you in my life, Sara."

"I am glad as well, but let's cut it with sentimentalities and look for something useful to sell." She wasn't about to forgive him that easily. In her mind, being and loving only one person was the sole way of survival in the harsh world. Philip's wandering spirit was too free for her, and she tried to use any means available to keep him close. "You know, we have to live off something, and hidden treasure is not going to find itself."

"I know, I get too lightheaded at times. But how are we going to get in? You think we should try breaking in through the entrance at the pedestrian bridge?"

"That's not a bad idea. Let me see if I can find something useful to break the barricade."

"I have just the thing, Sara." He approached the fence's remnants that once separated the road from the walking area and broke off a piece of rusted metal. Philip then waved the piece as an ancient swordsman would a sword, pretending to fight off invisible enemies.

"I am not sure that it will work; it is too rusted." She approached him carefully, as a hunter would its prey. Noticing he once again turned his attention to something else, Sara gently touched his hand then moved across until she reached the piece.

Philip's initial reaction was to strengthen the grip on his new weapon. But his instincts were powerless when it came to the woman he loved. Soon enough, he let go of it entirely and let her take it. Without a word, he moved away. He hated himself for allowing her to do anything she wished.

On the other hand, Sara's early exhilaration was replaced by sadness. She felt rejected, a fool for making the first move, for trying to connect to someone so self-obsessed. Anger rushed in, and moments later, she was at the pedestrian bridge entrance, hitting and breaking the barricaded doors. "Break, dammit! Break!"

"You are making too much noise, Sara," Philip replied to her, slightly raising his voice. "Someone will hear. You are attracting too much attention."

"Don't you dare talk to me about attention!" Every new word coming from his mouth made her angrier and her attacks fiercer.

"What did I do now?" he asked more calmly, trying to avoid an unnecessary fight.

His question caused Sara to turn livid. "Why are you so calm, dammit?! You don't even care about me." At that point, she resembled a wildling more than a woman from Old Vegas. Her fierce attacks caused the piece of metal to break, but it did not stop her. Like an Amazonian, she used her hands to tear through the barricade a make an opening. "Now that's how it's done. Let's get in. Hurry up, you slowpoke!"

3

Both of them were silent for an unpleasant amount of time within the remnants of New York-New York. Sara thought he was scared, and Philip didn't want to anger her even more, still unaware of what he did earlier. Even in broad daylight, the inside was dark. Only patches of light coming from the broken windows managed to bring some light and made the room slightly cooler than the outside. The place was as desolate and deserted as Philip expected it to be. Sara was aimlessly looking around for any salvageable item. It appeared their roles have reversed as they stood six feet apart, which was a standard procedure in case of unexpected collapse. They reached the broken escalator leading to the main hall. An empty, large room greeted them with open arms.

"I've got to hand it to those who constructed this place. Just look at it," Philip said, trying to break the tension that severely affected his ability to focus on possible dangers and probable finds.

Sara was silent.

"Hello?" Philip placed his hands around his mouth to emphasize the sound produced. It echoed the room and was louder than he had expected it to be. "Amazing acoustics. Just brilliant."

"Hey," Sara raised her voice, and the word echoed as well. Then, she shyly added: "Weren't you the one who told me to be silent earlier?"

He was about to apologize, but something inside of him, a sense of pride, did not allow him to do so. "I did it intentionally. As I said earlier, this place is completely deserted. If there were someone here, they would reveal themselves. "

"Or become more aware of our presence," she murmured. Sara then pointed to the only item remaining, a large circular structure in the middle of the room. "Doesn't it look like a pattern?"

"Yes, it does. Once, before the New Vegans took the machines, it stood in the center. It was a place where they served drinks. But the pattern you see was devised and built by humans. Like the Manhattan Express, its purpose was to free and entrap people at the same time."

"What do you mean?" Her mood once again shifted.

It was a pattern Philip knew how to exploit. Now that she was calm, he was free to do as he wished. "You see, it brought people into a situation with no easy way out. Imagine poker and craps tables surrounding the bar. It is very convenient to get there from any point in the room, and at the same time, it points away from the exits. People wanted to gamble and wanted to drink while doing so. Even if they knew when it was enough, they couldn't stop. That is how they were entrapped, allowing the system to squeeze every last possible coin from them. That's the catch. Let's get down and see if there is anything left."

Sara pretended to ignore him while he continued talking about different patterns he noticed in Old Vegas. In fact, she was intrigued by all of that. Unlike most men who tried to sell a story or create a fantasy for her, Philip deconstructed it all. There was no subject he could and would not talk about, no stone he left unturned. That too, she knew, was a part of his pattern of existence and used it to her advantage at times.

Philip entered the bar and pretended to be a bartender. "Would you like something to drink, ma'am? A cocktail, perhaps?" He was swinging an empty bottle around and poured nothing but the air in the two-shot glasses he found there as well.

"Well, thank you, kind sir. You know exactly what I need." Sara seemingly joined the play pretend.

"It is the job of every good bartender to know these things. Just by looking at you, I figured you were a Cosmopolitan woman. Or would you rather have a Martini? Don't tell me, I know. You need a Manhattan." He winked at her.

"Too bad we don't have any whiskey or vermouth here." She broke the illusion as she remembered what he did to her earlier. Sara was petty that way.

Philip, however, decided to take a different approach this time. "Let's go find some then," he stated calmly. "We have Times Square, Broadway, Wall Street, and more to choose from."

"I wonder if those places exist anymore. As much as they stole, New Vegans couldn't take the walls, the structure itself. What if the original city remained that way as well?"

"Well, even if it didn't, we still have their original designs here. We have the layout to rebuild when the time comes."

"Still, the world we live in today is a sad affair." She lowered her head to the bar, allowing her hair to cover her face. "Stupid me, thinking about the least important thing right now. It has nothing to do with our everyday survival."

"It has everything to do with it. Lift your head." He was unusually optimistic. "What's a life worth if we only try to survive, not live. Without imagination, hopes, and dreams, we are no more alive than those walls."

Sara was still facing the dust-covered bar, thinking of how weak she was.

"Here, let me show you what I found earlier." He placed his hand in one of the back pockets and pulled out a coin.

Sara was still disheartened, unmoved.

"Rise up, look at it. It is the real deal. I found it stuck in the escalator and planned to surprise you on the way back. But I guess this is a good time as any." Philip placed his free hand on top of her head to calm her down. He then gently moved it back, unsure of how she would react.

"What is it?" she asked.

"It is the original casino token, probably worth a small fortune. I want you to have it." He placed it in her hand.

A moment later, she dropped it to the ground. Sara didn't know how to react in such situations.

"No worries, I'll get it," Philip said confidently.

"No, sorry, let me take it. I let it fall anyway." Sara leaned back and bowed down to reach the token. That was exactly the thing she needed to bring back some energy. She noticed something unusual below the bar. "Hey, remember the thing you were talking about earlier?"

"The patterns?" Philip asked.

"Yes, the patterns. Guess what I found here. Spiders, a bunch of them. Just building their nests in peace."

"At least now we know there are some guests at the hotel." He smiled, glad that she was back to feeling okay. "You know, humans like spiders build webs. Instead of silk, we build them of patterns, trying to understand the world around us. Our brains are like cobwebs, a series of interconnected dots making a network. And each dot is one neuron, one emotion, one memory. For each person, that network is unique." He overdid it and was aware of that. His speech once again made her feel melancholic.

"Interesting," Sara replied. She returned to the bar and looked him directly in the eyes. Philip continued talking, unable to stop like a machine once put in motion. "That made me think. As humans, we do not only build the world inside our heads but shape the world around us. Look at the palms outside, burning up in the sun. They didn't decide when and where they would be born, did not choose to live on the Strip. They were forced there, much like humans within Zzones. All a part of a greater design." He felt like saying something more but stopped.

"I don't know how they survived for so long. I don't know how we survived so far." She paused for a second. "And you know what? Whenever I look at those trees outside, I feel sorry for them. They have to survive harsh conditions, and the fruits, the seeds dry up, fall, and crumble into dust. Whoever designed that must have been a terrible person."

"Do you ever think they feel sad because of that?" he asked.

"They are trees; they have no emotions. They have no choice but to grow where they are planted. It is all the cursed pattern." Sara was turning emotional again.

"Of course they don't. But they are alive. We are alive, and we have a choice. We are here, so we might as well live. Now let me pour you a real drink."

Lizard

The unsustainable way of food production before the Greatest War was named one reason the Old World ended. It was said that it caused the diseases that plagued humanity until its bitter end. In essence, even though many strides were made to alleviate the pressure on Earth's limited resources and climate, they proved to be insufficient.

The human diet, such as it was for countless millennia, could not be so easily changed without the change in humans themselves. For centuries great thinkers, philosophers, sociologists, politicians, and like-minded people tried to shape human conscience to pacify the vile nature of our soul. Yet no force was as strong as starvation in doing that. Hunger brings about the worst and the best in us. It peels off the layers of social norms, beliefs, ideas, and thoughts and leaves only what there always was, the instincts. Yet, no matter how difficult of starvation specific populations faced, global trends carried on. And when the globalized culture such was the Old World collapsed, there was hunger everywhere. For that and many other reasons, people died.

But humanity survived and needed to change, more than ever in its entire history. The end of the Old World perfectly coincided with Zetwork's plan to revive the ancient human species as most of them relied heavily on a plant-based diet. Its calculations were never able to fully account for human behavior variability, and meat production and consumption resumed on a smaller scale. Even in that regard, Zetwork tried its best to bring back versatility as one of the natural world's main pillars by reviving ancient animals that roamed the planet when human civilization first appeared. So many creatures were resurrected and released into a world that was radically different from the one their ancestors inhabited. In such a desolate and irradiated place, only survival instincts and genetic modifications kept them from becoming extinct again.

Yet, for the most part, the human diet changed to be more vegetarian. Plant-based products that already existed in the Old World were pushed to their limits. Zetwork emphasized the use of algae and other lesser-known and used species that did not require many resources to grow. As the population began to grow again, reliance on plants alone for diet was not enough. Humans, like pandas, were not very efficient in digesting plant fiber and extracting energy from it. They required protein.

Insects were a staple in the Zzones with once large populations and urban areas as their growth needed very little space and resources. That is why most pre-war cities that were spared the bombs began producing them. Once used for housing and business, tall skyscrapers were turned into refineries with various insects taking up different floors for better optimization. With many species and their waste products flowing down, they resembled tropical rainforest layers. Zetwork, than inorganic and artificial life-form, surprisingly found much of its inspiration in nature.

Naturally, such a large number of insects confined in small spaces attracted predators. The only predators large enough to have survived the Greatest War were lizards. At first, regarded as pests, lizards proved to be a natural source of protein. But before they were hunted to extinction, the United Zzone Federation brought a law to conserve and maintain their population. As per Zetwork's advice, UZF began experimenting on lizards with a higher survival rate in the contaminated areas. Initial findings pointed out that their relatively primitive bodies could be modified to sustain and absorb some radiation, which allowed them to be released into what remained of nature now called the Oblivion. Further studies pointed out another benefit of lizards, their tails.

The unsustainable food practices of the Old World were not only unreasonable and harmful to the environment, but they were also vicious and unnecessarily cruel. Animals were slaughtered without understanding or purpose other than to feed humans. Thanks to their evolutionary adjustments from eons ago, some lizards could detach their tails and regrow them. Humans used this ability to enhance their bodies, but after a couple of horrific accidents, they gave up on the idea. Yet they found use in their body parts, skin for protection and healing of wounds and the flesh as nutrition.

The practice of using lizards as food rose steadily over the years. It coincided with the main ideas UZF and Zetwork envisioned for humanity. It was sustainable as lizards ate the insects; they did not require a lot of other nutrients. They could regrow their tails in a reasonable amount of time, saving time and effort to grow another specimen completely. Such an approach was also cheaper and less cruel than other meat production methods employed in the past. No animals had to be slaughtered until they reached maturity and were no longer viable as a source of edible tails.

"Lizard tail is the new white meat," echoed through the Zetwork and into the minds of its users. "Try today and get a special discount on large quantities."

Yet human nature rarely changes to a high degree. What started as a project to peacefully harvest the lizards' tails was turned into perversion as the market demand grew. As humans did with many species in the past, they did to lizards as well. Torturing gave better and faster results as poor animals were forced to detach and regrow tails as fast as possible, similar to many plant species consumed for their psychedelic effect. Stimulants, though initially prohibited, found their way back into food and, eventually, humans. Food became more addictive and less nutritious. The wheel made another turn.

Countless generations later, these lizards no longer resembled their natural ancestors. Their tails were thicker, meatier, and juicier, making them appear like snakes. In certain species who could regenerate limbs, those grew out of proportion and turned them into monstrosities who could not survive without human assistance. And those slow, helpless animals were easy prey to the creatures who survived the Greatest War. And as the creatures changed, Zetwork, UZF, and humans changed with them. In just one of the many points in human history, the pendulum moved from one side to the other and back again.

On a wider scale, what happened to lizards was only a portion of what happened to society in general. The world governemtnt used force to bring reluctant Zzones under its yoke and then apologized for it. ZZ insignia UZF soldiers carried was equated with Schutzstaffel or SS, UZF itself with just another colonial empire in history who used the war to further its goals, and Zetwork with shadow government plotting to overthrow it and enslave humanity. Still, this one-world government was here to stay and, in the following centuries, expand. Lizards were among the first animals taken to convert and inhabit new worlds, to provide a source of nutrients for future settlers. Some of them went through centuries of forced evolution before the human ships settled, and they didn't quite greet their creators with open arms.

Olympus Hill

First settlers to Mars came in capsules that could conjoin and form communities, but when the time came for the massive migration, a cheap and sustainable solution was sought for the problems future colonizers faced. Therefore, one resourceful entrepreneur named Ulysses Hill developed carbide foam that provided insulation and protection from outside elements such as radiation, vacuum, and dust particles. He decided to personally test the invention by choosing a location far from the habitable zone to land. Out of many proposed solutions, he chose Olympus Mons; more precisely, he desired to bore a hole deep inside it and reach one of the newly discovered caves. To do that, he decided to make his spacecraft into a drill to enter a crevice in one of the volcano's older calderas. Whether it was because of practicality, his visions of grandeur, bold and uncompromising nature, or pure lunacy, no one could tell.

Ulysses was not alone in his aspirations as interest in Mars only grew larger by the years. What made him so successful was not his smart investments or connections, not even his hard-working lifestyle. It was his optimistic nature and outward personality. Many have described him as a man who always smiles. He was destined to transform this arid terrain into a lush landscape, and in his own words, "every successful project has to start from the foundation and build upwards, from roots to branches." His choice of location made sense in that regard, and he said his craft "would be the seed that will make Mars flourish." Using contemporary advancements like self-replicating nanobots made this claim a realistic possibility.

His project received attention from world leaders who understood the situation on the planet was becoming dire, and as a drowning man catches at a straw, so did they invest in his idea. It had sound physics behind it and its simplicity added to the success. Ulysses himself surmised the situation, saying that "we have to protect the Earth from inevitable destruction caused by global warming. They think tents and domes will protect us, but they will only delay the inevitable." Even with many world leaders' support, he barely made enough money to finish the project and start the journey that proved to be his last.

Resembling a heavenly needle, the spacecraft pierced the sky above the thin Martian atmosphere as it made its way to the caldera named in man's honor Hill caldera. When its destination was only a few kilometers away, the craft sped up instead of slowing down. The impact was not as magnificent or perfect as many have believed it would be. Instead, with lots of vibrations and grinding noises, the drill in the front broke through the surface. In surprisingly little time, he reached the destination. When he looked outside the ellipsoid window, he had a sight to see. The cave looked like nothing more than a hole in the ground to the unaccustomed eye, but it seemed overly familiar to Ulysses.

Even before going out, he saw himself transforming this hostile environment into a paradise of his own creation. First, he would use the foam to seal off any holes through which the air might leak out. As the cave was enormous, he would divide this task into phases, creating individual and independent segments. Then he would activate the electricity-generating system, which consisted of solar panels from the bottom of the rocket now at the top and on the planet's surface. For this first phase, not much energy was needed as he was protected from the elements by a massive rock layer.

The next phase involved using self-replicating nanobots to create primary machines, install lights, and activate robots he already brought. With that finished, he could focus on planting bioengineered crops specially designed for this occasion. The third phase of the plan involved sending the resources through the spacecraft to the colonizers nearby. Finally, he would invite the settlers to join him and slowly build and live in the surrounding segments. More space would be created for new settlers after those initial steps, connecting the caves into one massive superstructure. And all of that thanks to this simple foam.

After establishing initial contact with the settlers, he felt relieved. "Everything is falling back into its place," he thought. Then he informed the Earth's central command of his success and waited around 13 minutes to receive a reply. He knew communication with them would be unsuitable and impractical but felt calm in the realization he was not alone. There were people in the colonies he could communicate with, and that put his mind at ease. Ulysses lit a ceremonial cigar to remember this accomplishment.

But his success was short-lasting as a sudden dust storm cut off his communication and destroyed solar panels. "What kind of a storm would form this high up the Olympus Mons," he asked himself at first. But with no way to contact the colonists, it would take days for them to realize he was in trouble and more than that to come to his rescue. Due to this malfunction, he barely had the energy to keep the lights on with a spare generation. All of his trepidations about Mars have turned out to be true. Enclosed in a prison of his creation, Ulysses cursed Mars, himself, and the world he tried to get away from as he pointlessly tried to break away the foam and get some fresh air. This initial survival instinct soon subsided. Of course, he knew well that what was outside was not only an inhospitable world but also the one in which he would die almost instantly if he managed to get through.

It was turning rather cold as the foam did not provide the degree of insulation he'd hoped it would. His breath was becoming visible, and he wondered why he never took up smoking. Even in that crucial moment, he could not stop thinking about the most menial of things. He puffed a few whiffs and said: "I would have been a good smoker," trying to cheer himself up. For some unknown reason, a cloud of mist formed above him as the air he exhaled did not have anywhere else to go. He jumped on his feet, trying to reach it, and went over it. The low gravity of Mars pushed him above. Ulysses hit his head on the ceiling and fell back to the ground, unconscious.

Waking up several hours later, he realized the situation took a turn for the worse. The plume of smoke dissipated but, in its wake, left a dark patch on the ceiling, seemingly harmless. It was considerably colder now than before, and he went back to the ship to put the spacesuit on but stopped. He noticed the foam itself has changed on further inspection, its chemical composition altered by the cigarette smoke. It was eating away at the foam rapidly, threatening to penetrate a hole and let the air out. After all, the air itself was in no obligation to stay within the bubble Ulysses created. "How could it be? How was I so stupid?" he said, hit himself on the head and cursed.

He never considered the smoke would be corrosive for the foam. "Why did I do that in the first place? I am not a connoisseur, only a casual smoker, and I haven't smoked for ages. Don't know why I even brought that thing along with me." Looking at the dark patch above, he smiled. "I am lying; I know why. I wanted to celebrate like a fearless man, a badass I always pretended to be. That is what helped me get out of the desperate situation I grew up in and wiggle my way through the social ladder." Then he sat on the cold, dry Martian soil, laughed, and cried for making such a fool of himself. He laughed because he realized he hadn't brought a spacesuit along. He never considered that he might need it, not with the revolutionary foam he created. And after all, they had plenty to spare in the colonies just a short while down.

Ulysses grew up at an orphanage, and even though he had other children around, he was always alone. He only had a creative mind to lead him. And it did, all the way to the top. Somewhere along the way, he realized he had forgotten for whom he was doing it all. But by that time, it no longer mattered. Ulysses Hill was the CEO of many ventures he created from nothing, companies that revolutionized life for modern humans. His hunger only grew as the years went by, and his goals became more unrealistic. Yet, no matter how far one goes or how much one deviates, he will always find himself right at the beginning. It is one of the few truths about being human.

Trying to make a final mental note instead of counting the minutes before the bubble burst, Ulysses contemplated growing up. "As a child, I was often punished by being isolated, and throughout my life, I have isolated myself from others with work and my inflated ego. Even now, I have managed to get myself locked away without the possibility of escaping. Most would find themselves in the grip of claustrophobia, most but not those who spent their lives in enclosed spaces; those had to endure prolonged isolation. People like me."

He wasn't afraid of the dark, of the space closing in on him. Quite the contrary, he missed it and found its presence relaxing. "One of my earliest known memories was peering through the window of a kindergarten into the vast nothingness of the small town I lived in. This kind of memory persisted, and throughout my life, I found myself staring through the windows, at libraries, in buses and trains, study rooms, and later airplanes and workplaces. Finally, I was staring at the sky and what lay beyond it." The dark patch on the ceiling grew larger and larger by the minute.

"Though locations changed, my feeling towards windows had not. As a preschooler, I did not stare at other children playing around. As a student, I did not lament the boring and often complicated studies. As a traveler, I did not admire the nature around me. And as a businessman, I did not look down from the airplane onto the Earth below. Peering through the window brought me peace, a nirvana of sorts. Perhaps it was the only true enlightenment of my life. During the periods of mental exhaustion or stress, it helped me not think and hit the snooze button. Then why is it I remember those moments now? Shouldn't my whole life cross my eyes now when it is about to end?" He looked at the dark patch again; it resembled a window, a black hole into another universe.

Then Ulysses Hill rose, turned around and took one last long look in the mirror-like surface of the rocket, and realized he hadn't changed at all from that child in the orphanage. He failed in his quest to make an impact on society, after all. He smiled at it, in the most innocent way any living person could, lay on the ground and stared at the dark patch. "It's funny how people say follow the light. When I see the first rays of faint light or probably before it, I know I will be gone. "He embraced the cold, dark ground with his hands and made it his own. He knew that death would release him of his pain, as in it all are equal.

Panem et circenses

"Are you ready for the next one, cadets?" the officer asked, not expecting a reply.

"Sir, yes, sir!" an almost unanimous reply arrived. Two dozen students from the safety forces training program present in the room focused their sights on the living wall in front of them. The holowall presented a scene from one of the events held at the partly reconstructed Allegiant Stadium. Originally built to host sporting events, the once domed construction was damaged during the Greatest War. Used as shelter by some, home for many more, and playground for children and hunting grounds, it was from time to time brought back to its original purpose.

"Bread and circuses. Bread and circuses, cadets, is what our leaders try to use to bring the world and the human species from the brink of destruction. The wounds from the violent past still haven't fully healed, other human species are yet to fully integrate into our society, and the Zzone system is not yet perfected. It feels as though we are rushing towards unification. Is this the right time, you may ask? I am not sure as well, but this is our task. So, look closely at the presentation in front of you. I will ask you to describe it later."

The holowall shone in very bright light, then changed colors as it created images from thin air. In essence, the holographic technology used was very similar to that of lasers, just more accurate, made to cheat human eyes with extreme precision. Cadets put on their headsets with integrated displays for better viewing. Moments later, it turned into a full-blown simulation. A football field partly covered by a damaged roof was filled with players from two opposing teams. More than a thousand people filled the first couple rows of the seating area. It was assumed that the stadium was once able to hold more than sixty-five thousand people. Even with so few of them, the roaring and cheering were deafening.

Cadets were able to manipulate their personal view of the event using their hands. While most of them focused on the sporting event itself, trying to find who was in the focus of the fans' attention, one was paying particular attention to the crowd. Matias Rivera was trying hard to locate individuals he believed were leading them.

"Cadet Rivera, you have something to say about this?"

"Banana-brains, sir. They are all banana-brains." Matias, though interrupted in his thoughts, managed to answer in a calm and collected manner.

"What makes you say that?" The officer was surprised by this answer and felt a slight twitching in his left cheek. Still, he managed to keep his serious expression.

"By the way they behave. It is only a matter of time until the situation escalates, and the two opposing sides either attack each other or, unable to do so, turn their anger towards the players and judges."

"Anyone else?" Hearing no reply, the officer decided to pause the simulation just before the central part. "Throughout human history, the most effective way of crowd control was adrenaline. Aspiring leaders used to and still target that most primitive, animalistic part of the brain to trigger the desirable reaction." His students seemed confused by these statements—all but one.

"But sir," one other student tried to utter. "We are not officers yet. We can't possibly know that."

"No buts, cadet Nguyen. This is no game. Do not forget why you are here. This is only the first part of your training. Now continue watching."

The holowall sprung back to life, and the match resumed. As the crowd continued to chant, more cadets focused their attention on them. They marked individuals of special interest, leaders of the raiders who incited rebellious behavior. Using makeshift instruments, these individuals positioned themselves at the center of the crowd like ancient field musicians; the rhythmic beating, combined with their flaming speech, heated the situation even further. When it reached the breaking point, the officer once again stopped the recording to make one of his speeches.

"These kinds of situations will continue to happen, no matter how stable and prosperous our Zzone or the world is. But flaming speech on its own is not enough to incite a riot. Out of context, it is meaningless. As future political leaders, you need to learn from every source of how power works. These leaders know exactly how to control a mindless mass properly. Timing is everything, combined with loud noises that temporarily deafen and blazing torches that blind the unsuspecting victims. They overwhelm the senses, cloud the judgment, and reduce clarity."

"But sir, I mean, just sir, we are enrolled in this program to bring prosperity to every human being, Sapien, Neanderthal, Denisovan, or Floresian. Our society has learned from our past mistakes that destroyed the world. Now we strive to bring equality and justice to all." Cadet Nguyen spoke those words with pride in her voice.

"You memorized it perfectly, didn't you, Nguyen? This is reality, not a political campaign. Leave that speech to your superiors. Cynics would say we desire the power for ourselves as if we lived in a totalitarian society where despair and hopelessness rule. We aren't." He then adjusted the image on the holowall to appear smaller and further away. "This would make it acceptable to commit acts of vandalism and destruction as those are the only way to vent such an amount of pent up anger. I ask you all to think more about why you are here. Put yourselves in their shoes, become one of the roaring fans, one of the those who struggle to survive every way."

Everyone stared at him blankly, as if they were unaware of what he was trying to say.

"Let's change the approach. I will become one of the people in the crowd and tell you how I feel, so you know how you should or should not feel." The officer moved closer to the hologram, eventually becoming a part of it. His appearance changed, and the look on his face suggested he was doing something he enjoyed. Then, in a voice entirely unlike his own, he continued. "I had more important things to do today. But finding myself surrounded by this mindless mass, I cannot help but feel the excitement. They are unaware of the fact I do not belong to their faction. Not that

I belong to the other faction as well. Being factionless is more despicable and sinister to the mindless mass that cannot comprehend such a notion, so I have to choose a side, wear a color, sing a song."

Cadet Nguyen was about to utter something, and Cadet Rivera stopped her by gently touching her hand. "Don't, just don't. Listen to what he has to say." His whispering voice made her tremble. His touch on her skin made the hairs on her hand rise. From that point on, she found it harder to focus on the officer.

"At any given moment, these wild things would be willing to hurtle themselves down the flight of stairs if only hinted to do so and start a riot. Who is it that observes the game? Officers? Judges? Even the players can't help but focus their attention on the leaders. They are the stars of this show, and they know it; they feel it. The beat has risen, the rhythm fastened. There is electricity in the air. Everyone is waiting for something, some spark to light the fuel of burning desire and begin the carnage."

"I am sorry," cadet Nguyen whispered back to cadet Rivera. "I should know better than that."

"Don't worry, you are doing great," he replied.

"Cadet Rivera, I think I warned everyone, including you, not to interrupt," the officer, who was finishing his soliloquy, snapped. "This is the final warning. One more word from me, and you are out."

Cadet Rivera wanted to reply with a determinant "yes sir!" and barely stopping himself from doing so.

"Sorry," cadet Nguyen showed using sign language. She, too, knew that if she said a single word, she would be out.

"As my impression was ruined, I will go back to observing the same way you do. I will take your questions later." He stepped back from the holowall and to his original position. "In the pauses between dramatic innuendos, clapping and cursing are what keeps the crowd going. This mass cannot stand idle for long; without orders, their energy would dissipate soon. Therefore, as soon as the critical mass is achieved, they spring into action, break chairs, or anything around them and provoke the other faction. Younger and inexperienced individuals demonstrate their courage by burning flares and breaking additional chairs. They do not realize that even though this gives them freedom and power, they are prisoners, creators of their demise. They are controlled by the leaders who never extinguish the flame of hatred. While ordinary men and women love and suffer for their club and worship it, their leaders' eyes shine with different aspirations. Power, unlimited and uncontrolled power. That is the real danger, cadets."

He paused for a second, letting that thought sink in. "Those who seek brute, physical power end up on the other side of the law. It is an easier and much more dangerous way to express power. It takes certain intelligence to understand that kind of life. Though tempting and fulfilling, such power is short-lived. Those smart enough understand that to attain the power they need to become the law. It is no wonder many successful politicians in the past and Zzone Overlords were hooligans and team leaders first. Now we come to the point of today's lecture. To know how to control the people, you must be one of them. Don't think that the fact you come from rich families means anything. It doesn't. And if you fail here, it will reflect poorly on me, the Zzone, United Zzone Federation, and the world."

Only cadet Nguyen felt the need to correct the officer but decided not to. Cadet Rivera held her hand as they discovered a new connection between them, a source of might more potent than any physical strength.

The class continued with the cadets asking him questions. He replied as best he could, showing the rest of the simulation. To conclude, he gave a short speech on why the situation in Old Vegas is turning violent. "Ever since the murder of their leader, they began to call Ed the Uniter, the situation has been uneasy. Due to their constant ravaging behavior, the authorities are planning to construct a wall. This wall will separate them from the remainder of our Zzone to protect both them and us. It is up to you to make that transition peaceful. Be careful not to end on the other side. Class dismissed."

Planters

The Greatest War took our best and brightest. I lie. They died shortly before it. If they were alive, this war might never have happened. The Yawn virus was swift and deadly. After emerging somewhere in Southeastern Asia, it quickly took over the world. Only those isolated enough had the time to gain immunity naturally. It helped that at the time, I was working in a nuclear powerplant, a place with very few living things and far from civilization. Also, there is radioactivity that kills most living things. Several people in my plant eventually caught the disease, but it was no longer important by then. The world had ended in a fiery dance of atomic bombs, and surprisingly enough, the nuclear powerplant I worked in was one of the places that survived. It was, after all, built to withstand similar events. Just minutes after the bomb fell, our electric grid suffered a catastrophic failure. Everyone knew it was about to happen. There was nothing we could do to stop, only minimize the damage.

The initial shock pushed everyone into survival mode, but people started thinking about what to do next after everything went silent. Some maintained hope that the world would carry on as it was; others pretended they knew what would happen all along. I can remember their statements, word by word, as they remained etched in my memory.

"Everything will be alright. We just need to patch things up and rebuild, "Mr. Mckinney, an elderly site manager, repeated as if on a loop.

"You could have guessed something like this was coming. The world was falling apart for decades, climate change, wars, diseases. I wish we had prepared better for this." Mr. Dalipi, a brilliant young immigrant scientist, added.

"You can never be fully prepared," Ms. Rios, who has gone through much trouble in her homeland, knew what it meant to be in a dire situation. "We have to deal with what we have, adapt, and survive."

"No, in this situation, our only obligation is to ourselves." It was Mr. Moreau who insisted this was no time to be selfless. And he almost immediately proved he meant what he said. Mr. Moreau took one of the suits, some supplies and left. That was the last time we saw him.

"People, people, calm down. We are scientists. We must think about the short-term and long-term effects of what has happened. Now, we know how much radiation a human body can take. Judging by the wind, the fallout will not reach this area, so we are the lucky ones. We need to measure how much of it is out there, find safe zones, and warn people." Once again, Ms. Rios was the voice of reason. Mr. Mckinney and I agreed with her statement.

"And what about habitability?" Mr. Dalipi asked. "We need to have this organized, and we are out of resources, manpower, and general overview of the situation. There must be someone remaining we can contact to coordinate this effort."

For some time, the discussion carried on as the plumes of smoke covered the sky with no way of knowing if they would ever recede. With no contact from the authorities, we had to organize ourselves and make up a survival plan. My colleagues and I stayed in the relative safety of the powerplant until we ran out of food. That is when we were forced to look for it elsewhere. But before we could do that, we had to make sure no one else would be harmed. As nuclear decommissioning takes years to complete with the right resources and people, we could only manage to put the powerplant in the safe mode, an advancement made possible by the latest advances in artificial intelligence. We vacated the building after with only our protective clothing and tools. Our electric cars had a limited range, and gasoline-powered vehicles were phased out decades ago. But we did what we could with what we had.

The road to town proved difficult with all the necessary equipment shortening our range. We managed to find a supermarket close by. Some stuff was already taken, fast food like snacks and sodas were gone instead of stuff that gives sustenance. As the seven of us scanned the isles, we knew precisely what to look for, canned food. Some of it can last up to several decades. Thankfully, we had most of the other supplies ready and only took some superglue if one of us was hurt. We could use it to seal wounds in the absence of stitches.

The first issue was with finding enough uncontaminated water. As the power grid went down, the municipal water supply was cut. It ran dry within days. We knew there was an abundance of fresh water in the lakes to the north.

Our next goal was to find supplies from local hospitals and pharmacies. As we reached the city's remnants, we established contact with a small group of locals hiding inside a barricaded building. They told us the city was in chaos, ruled by local gangs. Radiation in the area was slight but still present. Laying corpses strewn about the streets represented another danger, not only because of the awful smell. They attracted wild animals and surviving pets who turned feral without their masters to feed them. Not to mention that after a human dies, infectious bacteria in the gut reproduce faster. We knew decomposing bodies could harm or kill us if we got too close. For safety reasons, we spent the following days with the group.

Antibiotics and painkillers quickly became the most sought-after commodity. Finding them was our top priority. With help from our new friends, we managed to get through one part of the city unnoticed. Words could not describe the destruction we witnessed. Feelings could and did. In such an emotional state, we arrived at the vet office. Pain reliever hydrocodone and antibiotic doxycycline were readily available, so we took half and left the rest to the group. After some deliberation, a unanimous decision was made to leave the town and deactivate other power plants nearby instead of staying with the group. It was a part of the original plan formulated inside the plant.

We knew that without electricity to cool the fuel inside nuclear reactors, the pressure would build up and cause the reactor's containment building to fail. This would cause toxic radiation to disperse within a fifty-mile radius or greater. Even a small chance to reduce the fallout represented hope for the future in an environment already poisoned by atomic bombs. As there was no contact from the other teams, we couldn't know whether they were still alive. So we headed away from what remained of Chicago eastwards, where other nuclear powerplants were located.

For the first few months, we moved down the Lake Erie, trying to stop radiation from reaching it and controlling the places it did. Charging stations began to fail as there was no electricity coming. We put up biohazard signs where possible and alerted the local population. During that time, there were very few hostilities, probably because people outside of major cities were less affected and better prepared for critical situations. We knew that eventually, we would have to settle somewhere. The only question was where and which areas remained unaffected. Besides that, this place had to be close to fresh, uncontaminated water but, at the same time, far away from major rivers. The fertile soil was also a must.

In the first year, we managed to visit most of the plants concentrated around Chicago. For those we couldn't, we received credible intel they functioned adequately with the staff inside. There was also a belated signal from what remained of UN, the world leaders in the newly formed Zetwork and their message of survival. We were informed that much of the work in maintaining the plants would be done by nanites. Next, they told us some part of the population survived inside the domes. Rich people, of course, were always better prepared for eventualities and had higher chances of survival. But our mission was not yet complete.

Our group foraged for food and prepared for the coming period in this densely populated area. Winters this far north were harsh; combined with the effects of nuclear fallout, they signified death for many. During that first of many atomic winters, many people died. Those who could not find shelter were affected by a combination of radiation, pollution, lack of food, water, and light. All of these factors contributed to the greater death toll. Even our group was affected when two renowned scientists packed up and left one day.

We managed to identify a few suitable locations for habitation based on the distribution of powerplants and the data we managed to gather about targeted sites combined with fallout predictions. Moving southward was a necessity, but so was analyzing the fallout reach in the area. Former national and state forests around Pennsylvania seemed like a logical choice, surrounded by nuclear power plants. When spring came, we marched back into nature, a group of five. Many feared us for the suits we wore, so they kept aside.

Along the way, we came across many people suffering from radiation poisoning. There was not much we could do to help at that point except offer advice and provide medicine.

After settling somewhere in what was once north-western Pennsylvania, we went looking for a steady supply of drinking water. One of the locals we treated told us of a reservoir that was probably unaffected. East Branch Clarion River Lake was one of 16 flood control projects in the Pittsburgh District. It was indeed fortunate to find a habitat near the lake. Water from it could be purified quickly and cheaply. The procedure was simple, boil the water, fill up clear plastic bottles, and leave them in direct sunlight for at least six hours. Since the sun was barely visible even during the brightest hours of the day, we used a liquid bleach solution to clean the water. The dam on the lake was yet another benefit. If properly modified, it could be used to generate electricity for our cars.

Farming our food proved much more complicated than that. As scientists, we did not need weapons. Yet, at that time, we realized how precious they were. Guns we found along the way or traded had another use other than defense and protection. We used them for hunting wild game for a while until it proved to be too expensive. Bullets were often more valuable as a source of deterring potential threats.

Farming proved to be a necessity, and after clearing a part of the forest, we had all the conditions set. Of course, that was beside the fact we had no seeds, and no sun was coming through.

We were not sure we would make it until summer. Yet, though not very bright, the sun appeared in the sky again. This simple everyday thing we took for granted just a year ago signified a renewed hope of survival. We also managed to trade some of the meat and purified water for beans and potatoes. Wild leafy plants and vegetables were already present around the edges of the forest. Cooked beans provided a necessary supply of protein, potatoes carbs, and leafy greens micronutrients like minerals and vitamins. A makeshift mini-hydro plant was constructed in a month and allowed us to produce electricity without solar panels. And electricity had many useful purposes, from charging our cars to storing perishable foods.

That is when the real work began. Knowing full well we would be unable to disable all power plants before they exploded by ourselves nor how long nanites could maintain them, we decided to recruit other people to help us. Our organization was named "Planters," and it had two primary goals. One, to train personnel who would disable the remaining plants, and two, to prevent further ecological damage by planting radiation-resisting trees where it was unlikely or impossible to do so. It was our responsibility for future generations and an obligation to those who died.

The United States had over two hundred nuclear powerplants, half of them built in the last thirty years before the war due to climate change. Now, fifteen years later, we barely managed to disable about a third of them. The further we go from our home, the more time consuming and complicated it is. Disastrous consequences of the fallout become more visible every year, especially on the children. Lifelong exposure to radiation caused their bodies to mutate. Mine started failing recently, and I am not sure how long I will last. But I know I have to keep planting.

Sapiens have returned

"The Sapiens are back! "one of the Neanderthals exclaimed. The whole village was staring up at the sky, looking at the drones hovering above their heads.

"Impossible," Joshua exclaimed. "It is not the time yet."

Their initial confusion was replaced by fear, followed by loud breathing, screams, and utter chaos as the well-armed troops descended upon the village. Rogues from the Great Plains often attacked peaceful Neanderthal settlers. These unsatisfied men and women came from the heart of a once most prosperous nation, currently divided into many parts. The northern, Nebraskan Zzone, never officially supported these raids. It did not prevent them, as well. The drones' misuse was also never reported.

Just before the raid started, the troops were given a speech. Their commander stood proud, observing his soldiers, and said: "In the past, we humans were alone in this world for a reason. We fought and won over those who dared challenge our supremacy. But today, we face a new enemy, the perversion of nature. These fiends have been stealing our cattle any chance they got. We are simple folk, and we do our honest work. You all know how hard it is to survive in this wasteland, the Oblivion. They want to rob us of our way of life and, in that way, kill us. That is why we have to kill them first." His heart raced as he expected the roaring mass to cheer and yell. "Are you with me? Let me hear it!" he repeated.

The soldiers clapped their hands in exhilaration, firing a few shots to the sky in the process. And so, the massacre began. They have released the hounds, who descended on the valley and chased the bisons away. The commander then climbed upon his horse and, followed by his loyal guards, charged head-on first in the manner of his ancestors. He knew it wasn't enough to murder the Neanderthals; they had to send a message to the others who dared steal the cattle or anything from them.

Quickly surrounding the surprised and unprepared tribe, the rogues overcame their defenses with ease. The commander asked who was in charge, and Joshua proudly stepped in. Other Neanderthal leaders stood in cowardly silence as he was chained and brought in front of the commander. "So you are the one they call their leader? Don't you know how much trouble and suffering you've caused? And for it, you will pay with your life. Kneel!"

Joshua spat on him in anger. "Who are you to tell me that?!" He tried wiggling away but the guards forced him to kneel before the commander, and the latter placed his boot on the man's face. "Know your place Neanderthal!"

It appeared that the more time passed, the clearer it was in his mind, an awful sobering experience to the reality. He smiled and repeated what his father taught him. "I had to do what I had to do, and you do what you have to do. So go on. Just know I refuse to die under your terms."

"You refuse to die? What impudence! Who gave you the right to speak!" the commander roared in anguish. He could not tolerate insubordination, even when it came from the enemy. He pressed his boot even harder to the man's face. "No one is coming to save you, you hear?!"

Simultaneously, a loud howl was heard in the distance, and the hounds who were chasing the remaining bisons pricked up their ears. Joshua used this chance to look for his two children and father as the rogues also turned their gaze towards the unknown. Howling of innumerable beasts increased, and as the commander turned to look, he saw a robed figure of an unknown person coming down from the forest.

The night before the massacre, the tribe celebrated with full bellies the return of the bisons. Months of famine have passed, and the radiation on the fields weakened by the renewed winds. Their nomadic lifestyle led them upstream towards the confluence of the two most significant rivers of the continent. The village traveled along the Great River for more days than anyone could count but with no animals in sight.

Like their ancestors, the tribe preferred to stay close to the rivers and forests, searching for food. Women would forage for berries and mushrooms, and men hunted as was the custom for generations. When the time came to fight and defend, all were prepared except for the elderly and children.

But now the bisons have returned. Big, sluggish animals were wandering the prairies, whole herds of them visible from a distance. Howling of wild coyotes was heard from afar, but no one had ever really seen them. It was said that they were heralds of nature's spirits. Only when they quieted down did the men proceed to capture and kill one of the bisons. They never forgot to honor the bison's sacrifice and showed respect by killing it fast. It was their way.

They have unpacked the cauldrons and lit the fire. The water, taken directly from the river, seemed pure enough to cook on. It was mildly irradiated, yet that was the case with most fresh water sources around the globe. As the hunters chopped large pieces of meat into smaller chunks for those who couldn't digest it properly, the furrier scraped the bison's hide. It would be used to make clothes and footwear. The children and the elderly were patiently waiting for the fires to flame to eat the cooked meat.

Old Connor was sitting by the cauldron, forcing children away until the meat was cooked enough and frightening them with stories about diseases uncooked food brought. "You know," he said, trying to sound rough but not overbearing, "I almost died of food poisoning when I was your age. I was hungry the same way you are now and didn't wait for the food to cook. I also loved the smell of sizzling meat, its sound, and its appearance. It made my mouth water. But it is no joke."

"We are hungry," the children cried in unison.

"I know that you are. I am too. We all are. Do you want to get diarrhea? Do you want your stomachs to growl in pain while you vomit the very meat you just ate? I don't think you do."

The children became silent, retreating slightly from the flames but still keeping a close eye on the meat. For a moment, he thought he heard coyotes again, but it was the tiny stomachs around him growling. Among them, he loved Shaun and Mandy the most. They were his grandchildren, so he allowed them more freedom with him than the others. Yet when Shaun got too close to the cauldron, Connor smacked him on the fingers. Mandy, fearing the same punishment, slipped away in time. Their father, Joshua, one of the current village leaders, was busy separating meat from the bones of the less popular bison parts. No meat was wasted, especially at this time. The long famine was terrible for the tribe.

When the feast began, Connor already felt content from trying half-cooked food and very sleepy. He approvingly watched men, women, children, and the other elderly treat each other with the best snacks. His head was falling, eyelids already blanketing his eyes. He didn't eat so well in a long, long time. And then, for no apparent reason, Connor's eyelids lifted abruptly. His neck elongated as he thought he sighted something in the distance. He was sure it wasn't old age; it was his experience that told him there was something or someone in the darkness. And it was enough to wake him up from his slumber. The moment he got up, there was a strange, short, and loud noise from the direction he looked towards. He shuddered at the thought it might be those he feared most, his life long enemies, the Sapiens.

Someone in a long, dark cape was approaching, almost invisible. It was nighttime, and no one could guess whether it was a man or a woman coming their way. The person stepped out of the forest as if it were a part of it. A moment later, after removing the hood, the woman's face became visible. She was young and beautiful, white as a pearl with long black hair. Her facial features resembled that of a Sapien. Just behind her, several beasts followed. They looked like wild dogs or coyotes, yet they seemed to be docile and peaceful, a cross between German Shepherds and wolves, der Wulfin.

Numbed from the drinks, people continued to feast, with only a few occasionally turning their heads and pausing between the bites, half aware of the strange noises. Several men reached for spears and bows, a couple of women for leather slings. The old man turned to them, raising his hands in a calming gesture.

"No need to be scared, not for now, at least," Connor finally said. This statement calmed down the tribe a little, with those previously unaware turning their eyes towards the unexpected guest.

"I come in peace," the woman replied. She was small and fragile, dwarfed by the size of tribes-folk. But her appearance gave out an impression of magnitude as if an invisible giant accompanied her. As she was getting closer to the light of the fires, more of her body became visible. Her clothes were not made of leather, not braided, processed, or spun, but of some smooth material no one in the tribe had seen before. She approached Connor slowly, her head held high as if they had known each other for a long time. Before the old man could speak, Mandy stood before him and raised her small hands in defiance, ready to fight.

"Stand back," Connor replied. "She is not our enemy." He knew that woman would have attacked before revealing her face if she wanted to do so.

As the tribe slowly gathered around them, the people, dazed and confused from drinking and devouring large quantities of meat, the unknown woman stood still, waiting. Der Wulfin, about twenty of them, imitated their leader but kept away from the tribe. Her gaze was fixed on the girl, as she did not find her appealing. Mandy was joined by Shaun, who stood in front of her, coming very close to the woman. He, too, was afraid, shaking, and it was clear he reluctantly decided to go forward. The boy jerked when the woman extended her hand to touch him, and he tried to get away.

"I've come to warn you," the woman said, pulling back her hand. "My name is…" Somewhere in the distance, lightning struck, completely unexpectedly at this time of year. Those who turned their heads toward the glare of lightning did not hear her name. Meanwhile, the children retreated, moving back behind their grandfather.

Connor recognized the name from the tales the old men spoke when he was just a child. "We welcome you. But you should know we don't take threats easily," he replied, trying to sound confident.

"I am not the one you should be afraid of. I am here to help you." She was now surrounded by the whole tribe, ready to kill her at any given moment. There was still not even a glimpse of fear on her face or in her voice. "Go away before it's too late. Otherwise, the Sapiens will come looking for their bisons."

Joshua interrupted, drunk and proud, stating how he could singlehandedly defend the tribe from any invaders, be it wild beasts or Sapiens. Others seemed encouraged by his attitude and dismissed the stranger.

"We are grateful to you, old friend." With a single look, Connor ordered Joshua to disperse. The crowd gathered around the woman. He wasn't entirely convinced that was the right move and wanted to avoid bloodshed at any cost. "Come, join us in this feast and tell us more."

"There is no time. I must go now," the woman concluded. And in the same manner she came, this unknown figure returned to the forest, followed by her der Wulfin.

The atmosphere was festive again, and they continued drinking and eating as much as they could. No one thought about the stranger coming into their midst. After all, there was no reason to worry about what an outsider had to say. They learned that long ago. Something did not let Connor be at peace. There were no Sapiens for miles around, not even villages or any sign of civilization. Only fields and forests spread as far as the eyes could see. Most of their encounters with Sapiens were uneasy and often led to arguments and general uneasiness. He remembered that at one time, they even helped the tribe on their way. He was still fully awake after midnight, expecting something to happen.

Before dawn, almost everyone was napping, despite the few who had drunk enough to feel free and roar obscene songs or start a fight. Connor was awake and quiet, and by the look on his face, it seemed he didn't get much sleep the night before. He was carefully monitoring the children, who, delighted to be allowed to stay up so late, were still asleep.

There was a loud bang, followed by a crunching noise in the distance. It was too quiet of a sound to wake the whole tribe, those drunk, too old, or too weak. And yet, every head rose without hesitation; everybody tightened, the babies wept. All eyes slid from Connor to the strange echoes somewhere far as their hearts skipped a bit. Joshua said that

it was the stranger who came back to tell them another story.
His father hoped with all his heart that was the case.

Yawnrus

Barely a decade passed since humanity faced its strongest enemy in the form of the auto-brewery syndrome. Yet a new enemy emerged to fill in the vacuum of power; enemy humanity could not fight, for which there was no cure. At first, its existence was considered a joke. It quickly became a thing of ridicule among the world leaders and common people alike. Some individuals still suffering from the auto-brewery syndrome dismissed it as a hoax. Yet this new virus exploited that very human weakness. A story about a couple struggling with it remained as one of the few reminders of life just before the Greatest War.

"Don't yawn. It's contagious," a woman jokingly said to her husband. They were in a car, driving back home. "There is not enough air inside."

"Sorry, I can't help it," he replied. "You know that it is in our genes, an instinct found in all humans. Maybe it served a purpose once, but now it is just an ancient evolutionary mechanism." Mark yawned reflexively.

"It will cost you, Mark. Guess who is sleeping on the sofa tonight. A hint, it's not me." The look on Chelsea's face turned serious.

"Come on. Yawning is a vestigial reflex. I can't control it, you know."

"I am serious. Vestigial or not, I hate it. Who knows what kind of diseases you have."

"But you are my wife. Whatever I have, you have as well." He tried to reason with her but instead managed to get her even more riled up.

"I don't know if someone at your work is sick. There are all kinds of people there. Plus, you could be cheating on me or something."

"Cheating? Me? Really? It's more likely the world will end tomorrow." He yawned again, too tired from the 12-hour workday he just completed.

"That's it, get out of the car. You'll have to walk home." Chelsea pressed a button, and the passenger door opened.

Mark got out of the car and waited patiently for one of the autonomous vehicles to arrive, which were the primary means of transportation back then. But instead of going home, he decided to stop by the grocery and pick up some supplies. He browsed through the selection of limited products looking for her favorite food. It has been a decade since yeast-based products were pulled off the shelves. Dark chocolate was the best he could find. On the way out, he noticed an ad for the latest antifungal mask and decided to buy a couple.

"Are you crazy?! I don't want to wear that," Chelsea yelled at him back home. "I wanted you to stop yawning. Masks are useless. You should have bought some yawn medicine or something."

"There is no such thing as a yawn medicine. I told you before yawning is not a disease, nor is it contagious. That is why I bought masks for both of us." Mark firmly believed what he said.

"Something is wrong, I tell you. I saw our neighbors yawning when I came back home. And then the mailman…"

"The mailman what? Don't tell me he yawned as well? Oh, you and your conspiracy theories. Haven't we been through enough? Just take the damn mask."

"No, you don't understand. It is much bigger than it."

They continued arguing until deep into the night and managed to agree not to disagree as no compromise was reached. The next morning brought some relief as they woke in each other's arms. The sun outside shone brightly, and the day seemed full of promise and hope. But as soon as she looked outside the window, Chelsea was horrified.

"Look at them," she told Mark. "Just look at them. They don't even have the obligatory antifungal implant behind the ear. What is it they think they are doing?"

"Come on, honey, don't start again. I thought we already put it behind us." Mark was still tired from a week of hard work and wanted to enjoy his day off.

She was right to be worried. If the scientists realized how the virus spread in time, they could have stopped the global pandemic. But if there was a thing the scientific community liked the most, it was percentages and probabilities. The yawn virus was just one of those improbable scenarios no one prepared for. And when it struck, it brought the world to its knees, like many infections that broke out throughout history. The virus took over the vestigial part of the human brain and forced people to yawn uncontrollably, thus allowing it to spread faster. For some, the scenes resembled a movie from over a century ago, invasion of the body snatchers.

They were not even aware of how easy it was for an organism, especially a virus, to evolve and decimate the human population. It's not that the human world didn't deserve what came for it, nor that it wasn't ready for it; most Sapiens were too proud to believe a microscopic organism would bring an end to break their perfect civilization. And it looked so naïve at first, a joke to so many. Yet, it was nothing more than one more result of the cause and effect principle. Antibiotics were used extensively in a last-ditch effort to get the world rid of SC11. They only managed to kill both good and bad bacteria, freeing up space for viruses.

"Yawning, when did yawning ever kill anybody?" Mark, like many other people, joked. If it weren't tragic, it would have been funny. But that virus somehow realized that when someone yawns, it automatically sends a message to everyone around them to do the same. Evolution. And it was the perfect way to expand. Scientists at the time could have prevented the spread of that particular virus, but with limited resources that were already focused on antifungal efforts, they had no time to react. No one believed the human race would fall due to a virus, among many other factors.

It turned out that it would, and it did. The Greatest War followed, and many future records claimed it was caused by one thing or another, each one appealing to the individual or group's preference. With it came a period of destruction, the demise of culture and civilization. However, humanity did not go extinct. Thanks to the AI network and pockets of people inside the domes, much of the pre-war society survived, changed, and adapted to the new world. And that has led to the development of nanotechnology, augmentation, and resurrection of other human species, among other things. The cause and effect law was not broken.

Made in the USA
Monee, IL
16 April 2021